KATHERINE PARR

Jean Evans

Jean Evans was born in Leicester in 1939 and now lives in Hampshire with her husband and two daughters. She was instrumental in forming a Writers' Group in Denbigh, North Wales, and is a member of the Society of Women Writers and Journalists. She began writing only three years ago and has to her credit several historical novels, amongst them RIVAL QUEENS, REBEL STUART, NINE DAYS A QUEEN, JANE, BELOVED QUEEN and THE WHITE ROSE OF YORK

FOR Jenny, Howell and Gwyneth
with love.

Katherine Parr

JEAN EVANS

SPHERE BOOKS LIMITED
30/32 Gray's Inn Road, London, WC1X 8JL

First published in Great Britain in 1971
by Robert Hale Ltd under the title ROYAL WIDOW
© Jean Evans 1971
First Sphere Books edition 1972
Reprinted September 1972

Printed in Great Britain by
Hazell Watson & Viney Ltd,
Aylesbury Bucks

ONE

LADY KATHERINE PARR, daughter of Sir Thomas and Lady Matilda Parr, fourth cousin to our most gracious Sovereign Henry VIII of England by reason of her ancestral descent from John of Gaunt, first entered the state of matrimony at the tender age of twelve. Her husband Lord Edward Borough, a man of mature years and a widower possessing several children of his first marriage, must have seemed an odd choice of mate to the innocent child who was thrust into his bed. However being a child of docile and obedient nature, the lady was never heard to make complaint.

The marriage in fact gave an added dignity to an already vastly becoming child, and it was not unpleasant in any event, she had to admit, to find oneself at such an age, mistress of so large a house and estates.

The strangest part perhaps was that the Lady Katherine should suddenly find herself step-mother to Lord Borough's children who were already well advanced into maturity. A bewildering position for any child to find herself suddenly mother to grown men. Indeed, Lord Borough's second son Henry was but recently wed to the Lady Katherine Neville, a gentlewoman of some twenty-nine years. It was as if nature had laughingly reversed the roles; and yet they were happy enough. The young mistress of Gainsborough, Catterick and Newarke accepted their teasing with good humoured patience and was much adored by the newly acquired family.

There were, perhaps not unexpectedly, no children of the union. Thus when the ageing spouse passed on, leaving the Lady Katherine a widow unencumbered by parental responsibility at the charming age of fifteen, she imagined reasonably enough one might suppose, that her duty in the bed of matrimony was happily ended.

The death of her husband however, left the Lady Katherine more than comfortably endowed with various estates and manors in Yorkshire and not inconsiderable moneys. It seemed inevitable therefore that she should not for long remain in her blissful state of widowhood, and the persuasions of her companion Lady Neville tempted her once more to look with kindness upon a suitor.

It was fortunate perhaps that the lady was not of a nature which demanded amusement and variety in her life. For this second husband, John Neville Lord Latimer was also a man of considerably more years than his wife who had yet to reach her twentieth birthday. The prime office of the young bride became once again therefore to act chiefly as nurse and companion to her Lord, and as mother and tutor to the two children of his previous marriage. This latter caused Lady Latimer no hardship since her own education had been thorough, and her feelings for the newly acquired stepson and daughter were in any event both gentle and motherly.

The residence of Lord and Lady Latimer was Snape Hall, an estate of considerable size which was surrounded by green park lands. It was but one of many properties owned by Lord Latimer which fell to his still comely wife upon his death in the year 1542.

For the second time in her life Katherine donned her

widow's weeds. This time the richer by estates at Cumberton and the Manors of Wadborough and Nunmonkton plus the revenues and all other possessions which had been her husband's. She was indeed a vastly eligible young woman. Of close kinship to the King and with wealth such as any man would be glad to lay his hands on. Estates and manors inherited from two wealthy husbands, added to which Katherine was also heiress presumptive to her only surviving relative, a brother named William, himself wed into a family of extremely high standing and close connection to the throne.

But possibly the Lady Katherine had had her fill of wifely duty, for she gave encouragement to no further suitors. Indeed it was many months before a gentleman received entrance to her small, close circle of friends and then it was for no frivolous purpose, but to listen to one of the many learned scholars whom she began to welcome to her house in order that she may hear them speak of the Reformed Religion. This not unnaturally caused a great deal of disappointment to her many would-be suitors.

The deceased Lord Latimer had been an ardent supporter of the Catholic faith, and as an obedient wife Katherine had followed her husband's views without question. Any doubts which might have entered her mind were swiftly subdued until now, a free agent in her own house, she gave ear to a number of teachers upon the subject of the Reformed Faith.

Katherine Parr, as she was again known after the death of her husband, was never to know what brought Sir Thomas Seymour, Lord High Admiral of England, and brother-in-law of the King, to her house. She persuaded herself that he came as a loyal Protestant, anxious to join the discussions which took place in her state chambers. But for the first time in her life her cheek flushed a little as she sat with downcast eyes trying not to see how he cast frequent glances in her direction. It was mortifying to the lady, an elegant creature in the black velvet of mourning, to learn that she had perhaps after all, feelings which could range beyond the gentle compassion which had thus far been required of her by two elderly husbands.

She turned her head away from the Lord High Admiral's gaze. Yet he found the delicate profile framed by the dark, gabled hood, infinitely as pleasing to his eye which was knowledgable enough in such things . . .

TWO

Tom Seymour leapt from his horse with customary vigour, turning the steaming animal over to the capable hands of a groom. He strode through the passages of Hampton Court with careless arrogance, as only the brother-in-law of Henry Tudor could. His cheeks were flushed and perspiration dotted the fashionable, short beard which adorned his youthful chin, and as always there was about him that vaguely familiar look which was a constant reminder to the court of his sister the late Queen Jane.

He strode towards the King's apartments humming a tune. Momentarily he paused, making a mocking bow to some pretty creature who blushed rosily as she sped by. Only afterwards did he recall that such dalliances must now be a thing of the past, for that very morning Thomas Seymour, Lord High Admiral of England had betrothed himself to the Lady Katherine Parr, cousin of the King. Even now he recalled the disbelief in those immense, dark eyes when he had asked her to marry him. And truth to tell, he was still more than bewildered by his own actions. That he, the most eligible bachelor at court should forsake his freedom for so demure and innocent a creature as the widow Latimer amazed him, yet he had been completely overcome by a feeling entirely unknown to him until now.

The Lady's response however had not been the joyous gratitude to which he had become so accustomed. In fact she had retreated swiftly from his arms, determined to recall to them both her situation.

"My lord, it is too soon to think of such things." Shocked, she had moved away, holding the heavy skirts above her ankles as she walked over the grass. His discerning eye knew that she went relucantly however, and he permitted himself a half smile as he followed.

"Madam, I would not intrude upon a widow's grief, but Lord Latimer was of an age to be your grandfather rather than a lover." He spoke with the callous indifference of youth. She turned away, apparently angered by his presumption.

"I think you mock me, Lord Seymour, and I find it most unkind in you to suggest that my husband's death means less to me than it aught. Lord Latimer was a most generous and tender husband." She retreated to sit nervously upon a bench.

Tom Seymour stood looking down at her, delighting in the picture she made framed against a background of early spring flowers.

"I intend no unkindness Lady Katherine." He moved suddenly, taking her hand in his and looking fully into her eyes. "But is gentleness the only quality you seek in a husband? Have you never wanted more?"

She pulled her hand away. "I have twice been wed my lord. The first was no choice of mine but I found no reason to complain. Lord Borough demanded nothing more of me than companionship."

"And at so tender an age you accepted such a fate willingly?" Thomas Seymour queried with a doubting smile. "Kate, a bride surely does not expect marriage to be nothing more than caring for some man in his dotage. Did you never hope to have children?"

Her brow puckered beneath the dark hood. "I was very young my lord. Possibly very naïve. I did not at that time give thought to such things."

"And the second marriage?"

"That was indeed my own choice, aided possibly by the entreaties of Lady Neville for her relative I will admit, but I made my choice quite freely and was content enough." Her eyes flashed a little. "You try to lead me to say things which were never before in my mind Lord Seymour, and I beg you cease."

He rose and pulled her up close to him, finding her confusion delightful. "I merely try to show you that there is more to marriage than duty Katherine. Your feelings for me have changed since I first came to Snape Hall." It was statement rather than question and he pulled her roughly back to face him when she would have broken away. "I am not blind Kate. It is more than friendship you feel for me."

"My lord this is most unseemly." Angrily she tried to release herself from his arms but was held firmly and knew that her cheeks flamed with colour.

"Admit the truth and I'll pester you no further Kate." She glanced nervously towards the house, afraid that some prying servant might observe her in this situation. "I still wear mourning for my husband my lord. Will you have people say that I gave him no respect?"

A cry of exasperation broke from his lips.

"Kate he is gone. You mourned him well enough these past eight months and there is surely a limit to wifely duty." He kissed her suddenly, fully on the lips feeling her heart beat beneath the black gown. She twisted violently trying to free herself until after a moment her struggles ceased and despite herself she returned the kiss.

When he released her she would not meet his gaze. Her usually pale cheeks were flushed as she fell back a pace feeling dishevelled and thoroughly guilty.

"That was a most unfair act my lord."

He laughed, charmed by her innocence. "But you do love me."

"I have not said so."

"You think I need words?" He stepped towards her again and she retreated hastily, more than a little alarmed by the expression in his eyes. "Shall I convince you further Kate? Kiss you until you admit it?" He mocked her gently.

She gave a cry of alarm and put out a hand to ward him off. "My lord I beg you remember my position. I do not doubt your sincerity but there are certain proprieties. Whatever my feelings for Lord Latimer, he was a good man and as such I do mourn him truly."

Her face saddened a little and Thomas Seymour realised she spoke honestly. He made a slight bow. "Forgive my ill manners Kate, I'd not hurt you. But answer me this, do you love me?" He waited impatiently as she studied her toes which peeped beneath the black velvet of her gown.

11

"I will admit my feelings for you are such as I have never known before." Her brow furrowed and she seemed suddenly embarrassed. 'But I am near thirty my lord. How can I be sure that what I now feel is love?"

Gently he raised her chin. "As for those thirty years Kate, you are still innocent as a babe. Will you believe it if I tell you it is love? I am not inexperienced in such things." He saw her look of shocked surprise and added hastily. "It is not something I am proud of Kate but when a woman responds as you do, then it is no passing fancy. Most women at court share their favours without a qualm of conscience, I dare say most have graced the King's bed at some time, but their way is not yours Kate. You'll not give yourself lightly to something which is not for good."

Her sleeves hung wide as she clasped her hands together, considering him. "I could almost believe you know me better than I know myself my lord."

He smiled. "I hope to know much more sweetheart."

She found the less formal version of her name very pleasant on his lips.

"I want you to marry me Kate. Perhaps then I can show you what has been missing from your life until now."

Her lashes flickered downwards again.

"I am not free to consider another marriage my lord."

"Those weeds will be put aside in a few months Kate. I can wait."

Her lips curved into an unwilling smile. "You are very sure of me."

He laughed and caught her tightly to him again, his arm about the tiny waist. "I know you love me. Be as stubborn as you will sweetheart, but I shall persist until you admit it."

12

She did not doubt for one moment that he would, but it was not in her to act coyly.

"I'll not deny it Thomas Seymour, but I must repeat, until my period of mourning is ended. I cannot formally accept your proposal."

"No matter Kate, no matter. It is enough to know I am not refused."

They had embraced then. He smiled as he remembered it, and now hours later he could still recall the pleasure of her nearness.

He came to a door guarded by two sentries.

These gentlemen glanced quickly at the tall figure and stepped swiftly aside. That his sister Queen Jane had given the King his longed for male heir ensured Lord Seymour a welcome reception at any hour from His Grace.

Within the Great Hall, Seymour paused for an instant as his gaze travelled the length of the floor to where a huge, bloated figure sat wedged into a chair of immense size.

Henry Tudor uttered a violent oath as his huge fist swept away the physician who knelt tending the foot which was raised on a small, padded stool. The man staggered and fell, his feet tangling in the length of his robes.

"Get out," Henry's voice rose to a crescendo as he hurled a silver dish at the victim's head. The metal fell with a resounding clatter onto the floor as the man scuttled away. "Parry find me a physician who knows his trade or you'll suffer for it. I'll not endure the torture this one inflicts any longer."

The man bowed, concealing with practised ease a sigh of impatience.

Thomas Seymour watched as the miserable physician

retreated almost in tears from the Royal presence. He didn't need to be told that Henry's leg was troubling him today, his vile humour was evidence enough. Reluctantly he went forward, flicking with his gloves at the dust which clung to his elegant doublet.

Within three yards of the throne, the stench which rose from the King's person was already noticeable. Those open sores ran with pus and the leg was blackened by bruising, yet though he sympathised with his brother-in-law for the pain he must suffer, he pitied those whose duty it was to tend this ruin of a man. Henry looked up, suddenly aware of the scarlet clad figure and his flabby face lit with pleasure.

"Tom lad." A swollen hand was raised to urge him forward and Thomas Seymour made a hasty bow before hurrying to his side. "Where have you been lad, I've been calling for you these past two hours?" The King questioned him with friendly severity and the High Admiral's face flushed. He could scarcely bring himself to tell the King that he had been delighting in the company of a lovely woman when his Sovereign had need of him. He was saved a reply however. "The leg is bad today Tom. I felt the need of some diversion and your gossip was ever enough to take my mind from this cursed limb." Thomas Seymour lowered himself to the steps of the dais with a cheerful grin.

As a young man Henry had prided himself on his vigour and conquests with the ladies. Now, although he still liked to persuade himself otherwise, he was entirely incapable of giving chase to the fleet-footed women whose steps were in any event quickened, lest this 'destroyer of wives' should happen to cast a glance in their direction. The days were gone when it was thought fortunate to have the King's

14

'favour'. The King grunted and eased himself more comfortably in his chair.

"I will send my own physician to Your Grace. He's an able enough man."

"Aye good lad Tom." Henry thumped him forcibly on the shoulders. "I've constant reason to be grateful to your family."

Soft music issued forth from the shadowed gallery which ran along the side of the hall, giving background to their conversation. Henry's eyes misted with weak tears of self pity as he was reminded of Jane. Jane who had shared his love of music, and who had died in giving him his only son.

"I'm a lonely man Tom. Lonely and ill, oh yes I'll not pretend with you." He prevented that swift reassurance which was about to fall from Seymour's lips. "Incompetent fools practise their witchcraft on me, tell me the leg will heal. But look at it." He gestured with disgust to the leg which was the size of a treetrunk.

The younger man looked with genuine pity where he was commanded, before turning his head away. "Only a man with Your Grace's strength could bear it."

Henry sighed and reached for a glass of wine. He drank deeply, belched and stared down into the glass, his face a mask of pink, bloated misery. "What I miss lad is the company of a good woman. It's been too long."

Thomas Seymour choked silently. Not since the laughing Kathryn Howard had gone to the block, that adulteress with the brilliant eyes and much tarnished virtue, had the King been known to speak of such things. Many said he would never fully recover from the shock of it.

"It's been two years Tom. Two long, painful years since Kathryn earned her just desserts, and in all that time I've not so much as glanced at another woman."

15

The High Admiral fingered the collar of his shirt nervously. "It was a tragic business. Not easily forgotten."

"Never forgotten lad, never. That I could have raised such a one to be Queen . . ." He gritted his teeth. "God's teeth it shames me Tom, it shames me." A tear ran to the end of his nose and hung there for a second before falling to the padded green and gold doublet.

"But there was no shame for Your Grace in the matter. She was wilful, undisciplined and fully aware of the deceit she practised. Why no man can say how many men had been her lovers even before she came to be Queen. You were not to know. How could you?"

"It makes my conscience no easier lad. The King should never had allowed himself to be so easily tricked." He sniffed pathetically. "I must be getting old to be so easily deceived by a pretty face."

"If blame is to be laid anywhere then it is with the Norfolks who thought to further their own ends by the marriage. Your Grace had no choice but to rid yourself of the Lady. None could say otherwise."

Up in the gallery, a voice broke into gentle song and Henry jerked convulsively forward, sitting rigidly in his chair. "My God what fool is he to sing that song?" The words were hissed between yellowed, broken teeth, his body seemed to shake with sudden pain.

Tom Seymour recognised it well enough. It had been a favourite of the late Queen's.

"I'll have him stopped Your Grace." Already he was on his feet.

"No wait Tom, wait." The King caught at his sleeve. "Let him finish, sooner or later I must face the fact that she is gone." He slammed his fist against the arm of the chair. "Why in the name of all that is Holy did I suffer

16

such misfortune in my wives? Of five, only Jane ever gave me real happiness and she had to die." The King blew his nose vigorously and Tom quickly filled another glass with wine, pressing it into the trembling hand. "God's blood it was not right Tom. She had no right to leave me." As always Henry grew angry at anything which was beyond his own controlling. He gulped the wine, dribbling and staining his shirt.

Thomas Seymour swallowed hard. "It was a tragedy which touched many hearts."

He and the King sat for a moment, linked yet further by the joint misfortune.

"What did I do to deserve such ill luck in my wives?" Henry queried with genuine bewilderment. "You know how I put my country always before any personal desires. How I wed so that I might give the people an heir. Where does a man find the perfect woman Tom?" He considered the younger man thoughtfully. "You know enough of the fairer sex, nay don't deny it. Your exploits give me as much pleasure now as my own once did. Where do I find a truly virtuous woman? because by the Lord if I wed again it shall be to please myself this time."

"The King speaks as if his exploits were all a thing of the past." Assurances fell glibly from the High Admiral's lips now. "Why with a few weeks of care the leg will heal and then I doubt that any can rival the King for his conquests."

A chuckle rose in the barrel chest. "Aye it was a marvellous thing Tom to see a maid flash her eyes at me and then to chase her as she ran squealing away." He laughed at the thought. "Hussies the lot of 'em." His face tightened again. "Not that I took such liberties when Jane was Queen. In her I did indeed find the perfect wife. Always

17

so quiet, so humble. No need for such dalliances when Jane was Queen. But for the others, well you know how it is? A man likes to know he is a man." He gnawed uneasily at his knuckles. "Kathryn proved it to too many, and Anne . . ." His small mouth pouted. "Like her cousin she bestowed her favours too freely. It must have been a taint which ran through the family Tom. I should have been warned when I lost Anne not to have wed her cousin." He laughed crudely then. "As for that foreign pudding. God's blood, Cromwell did a despicable thing when he wed me to the Cleves' woman. The idiot did naught but stuff herself with food and grunt in that hideous foreign tongue. Can you imagine taking that to your bed Tom?"

Thomas Seymour took his lead from the King. When Henry's eyes sparkled with crude humour, he joined his own laughter to that other which echoed deafeningly through the hall.

"Aye it was a lucky escape Tom, that divorce which parted me from Anne of Cleves." Henry wiped his eyes on his sleeve and wheezed breathlessly. A ripple of relief ran through the court. As always my Lord Seymour's presence had restored the King's good humour.

Henry blew his nose and eased himself more comfortably in the seat which had been specially carved in order to take his ever expanding body. He patted the leg for a second, sucking in his breath with the pain. Quickly Thomas Seymour signalled to a groom who ran forward with a cushion. This he placed on the footstool and raised the King's leg gently on to it.

"Aye, that's better lad. I forgot it for a few minutes, and for that at least I can thank you."

Those replicas of Jane's eyes smiled.

"It is good to hear Your Grace laugh again."

"I know Tom. I know. I've been a miserable soul these past two years. It's been half in my mind these last weeks to wed again." His brother-in-law hid his surprise well. "Not that I expect to find anyone as perfect as Jane, but a Queen would at least offer companionship, someone to talk to, to laugh with. It's a lonely business being King, Tom. There aren't many of suitable rank with whom I may speak openly. I don't know what I'd do without my loyal brother."

"You shall never have to do without me, God willing."

Henry smiled, his lips quivering with self pity.

"But where do I find the woman to be Queen of England lad? Is there any such?"

The High Admiral grinned now.

"The choice I'll admit is limited Your Grace, since the courts have ruled that only a woman of untarnished virtue may look to wed with the King."

"It was a law well made. It protects me at least from another such as Kathryn."

"But it leaves very few eligible maids of suitable rank Sire."

"You would doubtless know much of that you rogue. Is there any woman in my court left untouched by your skilled wooing? Who's the latest conquest Tom? What's her name?"

Some warning instinct caused Thomas Seymour to hesitate. He bit his lips for an instant, suddenly reluctant to mention Katherine's name.

"The Lady is not at court Your Grace, and she is only recently widowed. I doubt that Your Grace would find her of interest."

But Henry was not so sure.

"A widow eh, and you're not wasting time in flicking

19

aside the widow's weeds I'll be bound?" He nudged his brother-in-law knowingly, but there was only an enforced laugh to greet his jest.

"The Lady still mourns her husband and she is in any wise no giddy young maid."

The King's grey eyes narrowed as he sat back and surveyed his friend.

"God's blood I do believe you are serious in this matter. Why you rogue, and you kept it well hidden even from your King. Tell me about the Lady, Tom. I would hear more of this jewel."

"There is little to tell Your Grace." His heart lurched sickeningly. "She is but recently widowed."

Henry chuckled. "But I'll warrant she still has her looks or you'd not be so eager. Come now, I'll not be denied. Let's hear of her, I may learn something from you yet brother, and it occurs to me that I might choose to take to myself a widow. The courts could surely make no complaint of that."

Thomas Seymour's heart thudded loudly against his ribs, his mouth was suddenly dry.

" 'Tis the widow of Lord Latimer, Sire. She is some thirty years of age."

"Latimer?" Henry's brow wrinkled. "Latimer? A Papist was he not? A man who chose to follow the Bishop of Rome rather than acknowledge our own right as Supreme Head of the Church of England?"

"Aye he was, although the Lady holds no such devout views."

Something was still clearly puzzling Henry as he pulled thoughtfully at the pale beard.

"If my memory serves me the Lady has been wed twice."

"That is so Your Grace. Her parents wed her to Lord Borough when she was still but a child."

"Her parents?"

"Sir Thomas and Lady Parr."

Henry's eyes flickered recognition and Tom Seymour felt his pulse quicken. This interest of the King's was too great.

"It is the Lady Katherine Parr you speak of Tom?"

He nodded reluctantly.

"Why you rascal. The Lady is distantly related to me. Fourth cousin or some such. I see if you have your way we shall be yet more closely bound by blood than ever. Is it not enough that you are my brother-in-law?"

"One can never be too close to one's King Your Grace."

"Well said lad, well said. By the Lord, I had not thought of the Lady for many years. She will be quite a match Tom. Her rank is good and I'll wager she suffers no hardship by the death of her husband? Latimer owned several manors."

"The lady is at present living at Snape Hall in Yorksire." He volunteered the information reluctantly since it was obvious the King desired the knowledge.

Henry nodded shrewdly. "A goodly residence. You've made an excellent bargain for yourself brother. I can almost find it in me to envy you. Indeed the more I think on it, the more I do envy you such a pearl of womanhood. Be in no great hurry to despoil the flower Seymour. Leave the widow to grieve as she wishes. 'Tis early days yet. You understand me my Lord?"

Thomas Seymour looked sharply at the King. He did indeed understand. He was being warned. Henry's expression met his unreadably.

THREE

WHEN THE King rode to Snape Hall with his escort of gentlemen, the Lady Katherine was sadly prepared to greet such a visitor. Indeed as she came forward to welcome His Grace, her face was alarmingly pale silhouetted against the black silk of her mourning gown.

A maid had run with frantic haste to the door of her bedchamber with the devastating news that the King demanded her presence. Katherine believed the child to have taken leave of her senses, yet as she observed the girl's distress it became only to obvious that here was no jest. The King was indeed beneath her roof.

"He entered the house without any warning Madam." The girl's voice quivered hysterically. She lifted the folds of her plain blue woollen gown and dabbed ineffectively at her reddened eyes. "Standing before me so suddenly he was that I could only believe my eyes played me tricks. I all but forgot to make my curtsey, standing before him like a fool I was with my mouth hung wide open." This last admission of guilt seemed to fill her with dread, as if she foresaw herself being despatched to The Tower for such a lack of respect.

Katherine's eyes widened as she lowered her feet hurriedly to the floor.

"But what can bring the King here? Surely he must realise we are unprepared for such a visit?" She groped wildly for the hood which was nowhere to be seen. Her fingers shakily smoothed down the waist-long hair and mentally she cursed herself for having unwound the braids so that she might rest more easily. Miserably she hurried to the door almost weeping with vexation. It was too much that the King should see her thus. "And I daren't even linger to change my gown or coil my hair."

The servant clearly understood her distress but could offer no remedy.

"He is an impatient man my Lady. Pacing the hall he is, demanding to see my mistress and Henry Tudor is not the one to be kept waiting."

Katherine pulled frantically at the latch of the door, then stood for a moment trying to regain her composure. "What will he see when he looks at me Elizabeth?"

What the King in fact saw as she came hurrying down the staircase, her gown rustling and billowing, was a creature of amazing beauty. True he could see at a glance that this was no chit of a girl, but maturity gave her a grace a certain elegance which was lacking in so many younger women.

Her dark hair shone, ravenlike as it flowed about her shoulders, and as she knelt sweeping a formal curtsey before him, his hands almost ached to reach out and grasp that beautiful mane. His throat tightened. Anne had had such glorious hair. Black as night. So black that the people had named her the 'night crow'.

"Your Grace." Katherine was saying now. "I did not believe . . . I thought there must be some error when my servant told me . . ."

"I trust we have not alarmed you too greatly coz. That was not our intent." His scarlet clad figure beamed down at her as he stood, legs astride, waiting.

Katherine almost gasped aloud at the familiar greeting.

It was miracle enough that the King should stand before her, but that he should call her cousin, a relationship she would never have dared to presume upon, considerably bewildered her.

"If Your Grace will take refreshment . . ." Her hand gestured feebly to the banqueting hall but he was shaking his head.

"We would take more pleasure from a stroll in the gardens Lady Katherine, if you will consent to join us?"

It was as she recognised, not a request which could be denied. Briefly her hands went to her gown. She felt so dishevelled. He intercepted her glance of misery.

"It is charming lady. We find no fault with it." And then he was waving away her ladies and his escort, and holding out his hand.

Blindly she gave hers into the giant fist, and they moved slowly to the lawns of Snape Hall.

The King's figure was gross, so that he did not move swiftly, and she noted how frequently he winced with pain. After one length of the rose garden, his face was dotted with perspiration, though no word of complaint issued from his lips.

"Your Grace," she heard herself say, "the day is overly warm. If we might sit . . ."

Almost with relief he replied carelessly. "If you are fatigued Madam I gladly consent to it."

She nodded swiftly. "I am not accustomed to walking without some covering for my head. The July sun is very fierce." It was poor excuse for urging him to rest, but he smiled.

"This bench will give you shelter beneath the trees, and we can speak further in peace."

He led her to a shaded corner where they sat together.

Wildly she sought for some topic of conversation but her thoughts were so disordered that she merely sat, meekly looking down at her hands.

"You must wonder Lady Katherine what brings the King to your house?" Henry was watching her long fingers which fumbled nervously at the fabric of her gown, and felt strangely pleased that she appeared so overcome. He had not dared to hope for such modesty and apparent innocence.

"I must confess Your Grace I am somewhat alarmed."

His eyebrow was raised questioningly. "Alarmed Lady Katherine? Does my presence then disturb you?"

She blushed and hastened to reassure. "Oh, no Sire. I am greatly honoured that the King should choose to visit my house . . ." She broke off feebly.

"But you can think of no reason for it, eh Kate?"

At the tender endearment which had become so familiar upon Thomas Seymour's lips, her flush deepened.

Suddenly Henry's hand covered hers and she jumped visibly. Her dark eyes flitted upwards to meet his.

"Your Grace?" She chewed nervously at her lip.

"Kate we share a similar misfortune you and I."

Her brow furrowed but she remained silent.

"We have both lost someone close to us. You a husband, I . . ." He lifted his hands in despair . . . "I a wife. Even more, a queen."

By now Lady Katherine's curiosity was greatly aroused. The King was not known to speak openly of that last disastrous marriage and she could in no manner see how this might affect herself.

"Your Grace was most unfortunate. I know how one suffers the loss of a . . ." dare she say it? . . . "a loved one."

The King appeared to find no offence in it for he sighed.

25

"Ah Kate. I was right to come to you. I knew a kindred spirit would understand, would see what loneliness I suffer."

"Indeed I do Your Grace, I mourn my husband. It was a tragic loss."

"Yet you find some conslation in the company of others?"

It was innocently said but her head jerked suddenly up, her face paling. What did he suggest?

"I have many good friends Sire. My life would be empty did I not . . ."

He was only half listening.

"You might perhaps in time even consider a further marriage Madam?"

She caught her breath. "It is possible Sire." Had he learned of her affection for Thomas Seymour and found some offence in it? "If I found a man with whom I would be content to spend the rest of my life. There is surely no sin in that?' Her eyes flashed with some defiance but he was smiling.

"Indeed not coz. It is a step I would most earnestly recommend. You are still a comely young woman."

She relaxed a little, though still puzzled by his questioning.

"I thank you Your Grace."

Henry's attention seemed to be lost in the garden for he looked away.

"It is two years now since the Queen died. You know of course how sadly I was used by that woman?"

Katherine nodded but said nothing. Such things were better left alone.

"I did think after such an unfortunate business that marriage would not cross my mind again Kate, but now . . . well I find my life lonely coz, I have many years left to me and I like not the thought that I must spend them alone." He turned to look at her again, watching the innocent concern in her face. "What think you of the idea that the King should take a new wife Kate? A new Queen of England?" His pink face studied her eagerly.

Her lips parted slightly as she stumbled over a reply. "But it is not for such as I . . ."

"Coz I ask for your thoughts on the matter." His voice rapped sharply across the excuse. "I would not ask did I not value your opinion. You will please us by giving reply."

She bit her lips, alarmed by his sudden anger. Why did he ask her such questions?

"Then Your Grace . . . I think if there is a woman worthy, if there is someone whom the King would feel content to have as wife . . ." she hesitated and he nodded eagerly, urging her on. "I see no reason why Your Grace should not wed again." Her voice trailed away. But God help the poor creature whom you choose. Her brain echoed the thought.

He was surveying her with a strange expression in his eyes and she looked away hastily as his face drew closer to her own.

"You know that such a woman would of necessity have to be of suitable rank? A King must wed not only for his heart's desire, but for the good of his country. The King's wife must be of good birth, her virtue unquestionable and her manner pleasing. I have learned to my cost over the years that the people's thoughts matter greatly in such things. They did not like Anne you know, and they were proved right. They never did love her . . ."

"A woman such as you speak of will be difficult to find Your Grace."

"How so?" He questioned her with good humour.

"Why there are surely not many of sufficient rank."

He considered that as if seriously. It pleased him to see her anxiety.

"I can think of . . . perhaps one." His narrowed eyes were observing closely her expression.

"But has the lady those other qualities which Your Grace mentioned also?"

"Virtue? Of that I am assured, for she is but recently widowed and her marriage I know was a good one."

"Then she and I are not unlike." Her lips curved into a generous smile.

"Not unlike at all dear coz." Henry murmured. "As to her manner and birth. Both we are assured are beyond reproach."

"Then Your Grace is indeed fortunate to have found such a jewel. Since you value my opinion Sire, I would say do not hesitate."

"You think so Kate." He took her hand in his. "You believe such a woman worthy to become my Queen?"

She laughed lightly.

"Does Your Grace think so, that is the question?"

"Oh the King is assured of it Kate. I was foolish not to have seen it before." His breath now fanned across her cheek as he seemed to draw closer still.

Her heart began to pound. Why did he look at her so strangely, with such passion? What sort of man was he to speak of his new Queen in one breath and to regard another woman with such obvious lust in his eyes. Yes it was lust she saw there in his ageing, flabby face.

She rose suddenly, forgetting herself. Pressing a hand to her brow. He sat watching the confusion which flickered across her lovely face, then he too rose painfully, biting back a gasp of pain. He stood before her.

"What troubles you Kate? Have my words offended?"

Swiftly she turned, her black gown rustling, swirling about her ankles.

"Offended Your Grace? In what manner may your words offend me?"

For a moment he stood motionless, a frown creasing his plump face.

"Have you not understood Kate? Have you truly not seen what I thought must be so obvious?" His hands reached out suddenly to grip her shoulders. She gasped with alarm, her eyes widening with fright.

"Your Grace?" Her voice broke in some unknown fear. "I am bewildered by this. What would you have me understand?" Her eyes filled with tears of vexation that he should find her so foolish.

"Kate my love, I am asking you to become my wife. My Queen. I thought you must surely guess."

For a moment her heart seemed to cease beating. She stared at him, the huge misshapen wreck of a man who had once been the most handsome King in Christendom. Years of excess in wine, food and women had taken their toll. Now his body, once so fine was bloated, covered with evil smelling sores. Why he could scarce move without crying out in pain. Her heart pitied him yet even more did it want to scream aloud the fear in her, that she would not become the sixth victim of his lechery.

"Your Grace if I did become your mistress my neck would surely be safer than were I your wife."

The sharp words could surely not have fallen from her own lips, yet as she watched his mouth fall open, she knew it to be true. Aghast her hand flew to her mouth. Dear Lord what had possessed her to say it? But the King was smiling.

29

"You fear my council Kate? Well sweetheart you need not. This marriage will meet with no opposition for even they can find no fault in this choice. You need not fear to stand before them as my wife. If this is why you hesitate then think no more of it."

Her breath came in short gasps. He had misunderstood, but still her fear remained. How did one refuse the King and still keep one's head on one's shoulders?

"Your Grace I could not become your wife. The Lady Katherine Latimer is surely not worthy of the title you would bestow." Her voice sounded strained even to her own ears.

"But you forget Kate, we are cousins. Linked by the very blood in our veins."

"But the relationship is very distant Sire." She protested.

"Fourth cousins Kate. Not so very distant yet enough that a special dispensation will not be required."

"I still wear my widow's weeds Your Grace. It is not yet twelve months since my husband died." Desperately she looked for some means of escape from this nightmare, but he waved aside her objections as if they were nothing.

"I admire your loyalty Kate, but a woman of such beauty and youth cannot mourn for ever. Your duty to Lord Latimer is done. Your King has need of you. Would you deny me Kate?"

Miserably she stared down at her feet. Tears threatened to fall and she swallowed hard, afraid to let him see what distress he caused.

"This is so unexpected Your Grace. I cannot believe myself worthy of the honour you seek to bestow. There is surely some other woman . . ."

His lips pouted in sudden anger.

"We do not look for some other woman, Lady Katherine. We have chosen you to share our throne. Think you we know not our own mind? We know you will not refuse the honour, being mindful of our wrath should you do so." Peevishly he hobbled round to face her. Furious that she kept turning away, hiding her face. "Kate I tell you this, I am set on marrying again and I have chosen the one woman I would see my Queen. In so many years I have only once found real contentment, and that with Queen Jane. She was taken from me and now I look to find that same happiness with you. I still hope for heirs. You are young we can still hope for sons."

Blindly she fought down her nausea, pressing the back of her hand to her mouth. To have sons by this man when she had allowed herself to dream of Thomas Seymour's babes, it was a hideous nightmare.

"In two marriages Sire I have never had any hopes of a child. It seems unlikely now . . ."

"With two such husbands Kate it is not to be wondered at." He laughed coarsely. "I still have many years before me. My body is strong, capable of begetting sons. This time you shall have a husband worthy of the name."

Looking at him she wondered how he could so deceive himself, yet suddenly she could find no more arguments. A deep fear warned that did she refuse it might not only be herself who suffered the consequences. The King was determined and no words would change that stubborn man who had always had his way.

"It would seem Your Grace is not to be swayed by my humble protestations."

She forced herself to say it.

"Your modesty charms me Kate. What good fortune that

31

I should chance to pay this sudden visit and find such a jewel."

Sharply she glanced at him and saw the faint colour steal up into his neck. How much had chance played its part she wondered, but looked quickly away as his face reddened.

"I'll not let you persuade me Kate. I am determined on it, you shall be my wife."

"Then I cannot refuse Your Grace." Tears began to run freely onto her cheeks and he took them to be tears of joy. Swiftly she curtsied, bowing her head so that he should not see her anguish. "I do most humbly thank the King for this great honour. I can find no words . . ."

"Nay Kate." He limped forward urging her to her feet. His bloated face was pink with childlike pleasure. "Don't kneel to me sweetheart. Such formality we will save for the court. Kiss me love. Kiss Hal who will be your husband as swiftly as I can bring it about."

She forced herself to smile while her heart cried out for the comfort of Tom Seymour's arms. Slowly she went forward, turning aside her head so that she might avoid those hanging jowls, the sour breath. But his arms snatched suddenly at her. His lips clung to hers and he was kissing her violently. Her first impulse was to scream that he stop, release her from this despicable fate, but somehow she fought back the panic. Her fists clenched tightly against his doublet as she allowed herself to remain crushed against his immense chest.

At last he broke away. Perspiration streamed from his brow, not even to himself did the King admit that the pain of his leg could now overcome his passion for a beautiful woman.

"I must restrain myself Kate." He gasped breathlessly.

He loved the paleness of her face, saw how she pressed a hand to her lips. What an innocent he thought with pleasure. Obviously she had never known such a kiss before. Inwardly he laughed. I'll wager not even young Seymour can bring such a flush to the lady's cheek. She'll forget him in time.

Katherine closed her eyes for a moment. Why oh why had she not allowed herself to be rushed into marriage with beloved Thomas? Were it not for her foolish resistance she might by now have been Lady Seymour, safe from the King's clutches. She realised the King watched and her lashes fluttered swiftly open.

"Forgive me Your Grace. I am still confused."

"Nay ask no forgiveness Kate." He said gently. "We understand but you need not fear, we shall soon be toegther always." His arms squeezed her tiny waist.

"What can I say?"

He took her hand, patting it gently. "Walk with me to the house sweetheart. I must return to Hampton Court but within a few short days you shall hear from me again. Prepare yourself to come to London, Kate, as Queen of England. I only wish I could stay longer with you."

"It is our misfortune that Your Grace must hurry away." She responded quickly. "But we understand the duties which demand your presence."

He congratulated himself upon having found so understanding a creature. They were at the house now and he called for his escort. Katherine's servants stood watching nervously as the King bent over Lady Latimer's hand.

The expression in Henry's eyes was lost to none of them, nor the familiarity with which he brushed his lips against their mistress's hand. Her cheeks blushed rosily yet the tears glistening on her lashes and the trembling of her mouth were evidence rather of misery than overwhelming pleasure. The maids stood watching with ill concealed curiosity.

At last the King straightened up and donned the green feathered cap which was handed to him.

"Till we meet again then sweetheart, within the week. If I can bring it about."

Lady Latimer fell into a deep curtsey, followed in the gesture by her maids. Henry's arm raised her again gently to stand at his side.

"Ladies, good gentlemen, I ask your homage also for England's future Queen, the Lady Katherine Parr."

The stunned silence which followed his words seemed uncomfortably long to the unwilling victim of the Sovereign's lust. She felt no pride in the sudden formal bows of the stunned men or the bewildered, flustered obeisance of her ladies, but merely a terrible fear that she had stepped into something which was utterly beyond her control.

The girl Elizabeth and the rest of her servants helped her to walk back into the house, supporting her numbed body on either side, though it seemed of a sudden that they were almost afraid to touch the future Queen of England.

She sat in silence at the highly polished oak table, seeing reflected there a pale face and recognising it vaguely as her own. Hysterically she wondered why it still looked the same.

"What shall I do Elizabeth? What can I do?"

The girl clasped her hands in the folds of her woollen gown, and stood shaking her head, hearing the cry for help but completely unable to answer it. She shrugged helplessly.

" 'Tis nothing new to be wed for an alliance my Lady. You've survived it twice, you can do naught but reconcile yourself to it again. The circumstances are not overly different, save that this time you will gain for yourself a vastly greater title. Women of my station never think of love. We take the best husband we can find and give thanks for it, though praise be my family will not see me go to some old man who looks only for a strong pair of hands to keep his house clean, and a young body to warm his bed."

Katherine Parr closed her eyes and tears fell from beneath the long lashes as the bleak thought struck her that it was to just such a fate that she had been condemned.

Someone placed a glass of wine in her hand and she drank it without thinking.

"I think I would rather die Elizabeth. If I could die tonight in my sleep and the nightmare be ended, I would ask nothing more."

"Nay my Lady don't say it." The girl was horrified. "Console yourself with the thought that this marriage will bring much advantage to your family, aye even to you. Can you look so lightly at the crown of England? Wave a finger at it and say, I'll have none of you? My Lady, women have died for such honour."

"Do you think I need to be reminded of it?" Katherine's head jerked up convulsively to the girl's miserable face.

"Nay it was an unfortunate choice of words Mistress. Forgive me?"

Tight-lipped Katherine merely nodded and rose, pushing back the flowing hair which covered her shoulders.

"I must send for my sister Lady Herbert. I don't think I can bear this alone."

"Perhaps Mistress Neville too my Lady, you always enjoyed her company?"

"Yes perhaps so Elizabeth. I shall need some help in any event if I am to go to court in so short a time." Abruptly she came to a halt, coming once more face to face with the inevitable. "I shall take my sister and Margaret Neville to court with me. If the King is so determined to make me a Queen then I shall at least use that title to gain me some minor privileges."

"He would not deny you the comfort of your own kinswoman I am sure my Lady."

"Indeed he could not child, since I think the Queen may choose her own household. My sister will enjoy acting as Lady in Waiting."

" 'Tis as I said there are consolations my Lady."

"But I would rather it fell to any other woman than I Elizabeth. I was not meant to be a Queen."

The maid flicked at a speck of dust. "And why not? The King is after all related to you. Yours is a good family."

Katherine smiled wryly. "Then I wish it were not. What knowledge have I of such things as a Queen must have? I was meant to be some other man's wife."

"Thomas Seymour's wife?" The maid added with a hint of disrespect, so that Katherine paled visibly and boxed her ears soundly.

The girl fell back with a cry. Not that she was hurt, but never before had Mistress Parr lost her temper and it came as a considerable shock.

"You will not speak again of my Lord Seymour, Elizabeth, do you understand?"

The girl stared at her stupidly. "Nay my Lady, I don't. But it shall be as you say I'm sure."

Katherine sighed. "Forgive me, my nerves are on edge. I should not have struck you."

"It doesn't matter my Lady."

"Yes indeed it does child. You shall not suffer for my misfortunes, but in this matter I am in earnest. You must forget that Lord Seymour ever came here. Ignore gossip which says that I thought to wed. Far better . . . far safer that way."

Realisation dawned in the girl's eyes. "You can trust me my Lady."

"I know it." Katherine embraced her warmly. "You shall come with me to court Elizabeth. Perhaps we can find you some pleasant young husband. Your parents will not object I think?"

The young face shone with disbelief. "How could they my Lady? Why 'tis surely beyond their wildest dreams that the Queen herself should make a match for me. I shall be eternally grateful Madam."

"Save your gratitude Elizabeth and help me instead in a more practical way. My gowns must be sorted, laundered and repaired."

"You will have new gowns, the King is a generous man in such matters we all know it."

"I am sure he is, but nevertheless I shall take with me my own possessions. I care very little for over rich gowns, jewellery and the like." A frown furrowed the smooth brow. "Doubtless it is one more thing I shall learn to accept. I should be grateful perhaps that my parents wed me to Lord Borough, it will stand me in good stead for yet another such marriage." She shook off the thought. "Have a man ride to my sister's house and bid her come to me as swiftly as possible. Let him tell her only what is necessary that I need her. The rest can be told later. Then I think we must set the household to packing my personal items. Linens, my books and a few jewels. Hampton Court will not suffer I think for my few little treasures."

She watched as servants sped away and let her eyes wander sadly over the familiar room which was no longer to be part of her life.

FOUR

THE QUEEN sat in her private apartments, surrounded by her circle of newly chosen ladies.

As yet Katherine had not become accustomed to the splendour of her new state. Even the elegant gown she wore, a crimson brocade, its sleeves slashed and puffed to reveal the underlining of silver and blue, as was the very wide skirt, seemed strangely out of place after the black which she had worn these past twelve months. Her dark hair was coiled beneath a crimson hood which was edged with gems. It was too rich for her own taste, but Henry loved to see his beautiful young wife so brilliantly attired.

For a moment, the book she was holding rested on her knees, and her gaze stared fixedly through the window. Yet her attention was not on the roses, nor the lawns of Hampton Court, it was with the King her husband.

The marriage ceremony was still but a dream. A haze which could not be penetrated. That she was at last Henry of England's wife only came to her when the King had thrown himself with suddenly restored vigour into the marriage bed. That night was one which Katherine Parr the Queen would never forget.

And yet he was kind, gentle, almost humbly so. She could make no complaint of his tenderness and childlike wish to please. These first few weeks of marriage left her merely with a feeling of numbness and the so often asked question, why? Why had she been chosen for such a fate to

38

become a Queen? It was as if her heart could not be moved by any emotion save pity for his pain and his obvious determination to prove himself still a man, capable of filling a woman with passion.

In the privacy of her apartments, the Queen had shed many tears. Tears of self-pity, of anger and disappointment. Only her close companions knew of those tears, her sister Lady Ann Herbert newly appointed as Lady in Waiting to the Queen, and the tiny Jane Grey, who despite her nine years was the soul of discretion. Only these witnessed the Queen's distress. To the rest of the court, Katherine Parr the King's sixth wife was a woman of extreme dignity, good looks and gentle manner. Not by a flicker of those dark eyes did she betray her grief.

One of her maids was curtseying now. Katherine recalled herself with a start to the present.

"What is it Jane?"

"'Tis Lord Seymour, Madam." The girl smiled. "He begs that the Queen's Grace receive him."

Katherine's face whitened with disbelief. Not since that last happy occasion at Snape Hall had she seen Tom Seymour, for the King had suddenly and without apparent reason withdrawn his favour. He had ordered the High Admiral to leave the court, and not even for the marriage celebrations did he return. But that was in some measure a relief, for she couldn't have borne to see him again in such circumstances. She frowned and the child Jane stood wide eyed and patient, clasping her hands upon her gown. Common sense warned Katherine that she must act with caution, as Queen her actions were swiftly noted and commented upon.

"He chooses a strange time to call does he not?" She put aside the book and rose unsteadily to her feet. "It must

39

be almost time for me to go to the King's apartment. His Grace will be most displeased if I am late for our game of cards."

"Lord Seymour appeared to be very agitated Madam."

Katherine bit her lip. She did not doubt it. But what on earth had possessed him to be so foolhardy as to return to court without the King's permission?

"Perhaps I should see him."

The maid stood silent as the Queen fought this battle between her conscience and her duty. Yet it was already decided.

"Show him in Jane. Since it is clearly important I cannot deny him audience."

The girl withdrew and returned a moment later followed by Thomas Seymour.

From where she stood, Katherine watched his approach. His tall figure strode energetically forward. A hand rested on the bodice of her gown as if to still the beating of her heart, his face was so dear to her, so handsome. Swiftly she pushed the thought away, raising her head as if to deny the weakness in herself. Her gaze met his and for one dreadful moment she feared that he was about to sweep her into his arms. Swiftly her hand was raised and as if recalling the situation he halted suddenly with a frown of pain. He saw the warning in her eyes and his head bent over the slender fingers, pressing them to his lips. Even this gesture was too much. Her hand was suddenly snatched away, and she saw the hurt look in his eyes, beseeching her to have pity.

Katherine's gaze flickered towards her ladies who bent swiftly over their embroidery again. Tom Seymour understood. She must of necessity act cautiously. He understood his brother-in-law the King well enough to feel pity for any woman who became Queen.

She was gesturing now towards the window.

"We can speak privately here my Lord." Already she was moving briskly away. "You have been away from court for some time, is your business now completed then?" The words meant nothing, they were merely sounds for the benefit of listening ears.

He nodded automatically following her slender figure, noting the gentle sway of the beautiful gown. To his eyes the change in her was amazing. She looked every inch a Queen yet it had been but a few weeks . . .

At last she turned to face him and he saw how she fought for control. Her eyes darted nervously towards her ladies.

"Tom have you taken leave of your senses to come here like this?" She was pale and faint mauve lines were traced beneath her eyes.

He frowned. Surely she had some better greeting. "Kate what happened?" Without thinking he stepped closer appealing for some end to his confusion. She retreated hastily in panic.

"That is something I have asked myself too often these past weeks." Her voice was no more than a whisper so afraid was she of being overheard. "That day when you left me at Snape Hall . . . I was so happy Tom." She swallowed hard. "If only you knew how many times I have cursed myself since then for my stupidity. If only I hadn't delayed our marriage . . ."

He watched her in silence unable to ask the hundreds of questions which crowded his mind.

"The King rode quite without warning to the Hall. Oh Tom, how naïve I was not to have seen . . ." She broke off quickly realising the futility of it all. "He began to speak to me of his longing to take another wife. Tom, I urged him to it. I who was so sure that one day soon I would become your wife. I didn't see what it was leading to." Her lips trembled as she tried to explain. "You must always believe, this was never my choice Tom."

"My poor sweet Kate." His face was white with misery.

She shook her head. "It is too late for regrets Tom. He was determined on it. I made so many excuses. I fear his anger was greatly roused, and in the end there were no arguments to offer. It was done before I realised, and I could only wonder why you didn't come to me, rescue me from this nightmare."

He turned away, thudding a fist into the palm of his hand. Silent fury and frustration welled up in him. "You must know the King well enough to know the choice was not mine. In God's name, how can he do this to me, who was his friend? How can I release you Kate, there must be some way?"

"No Tom, no. There is no way. It is pointless to talk of release. I am committed now."

"You surely can't be content to live with such a vile monster, a man who sets so little store by friendships that he will resort to this . . ."

"Tom." She frowned and held up her hand to silence him. "Can you not see. It is all too late? I am his wife a Queen however unwilling. Can you not imagine what fate we would both suffer if the King should even suspect what is between us? Have you even given thought to how he will receive this most foolish return to court?"

"As to that I was beyond caring. But I think even the King cannot deny me the right to attend to my own estates occasionally, and since I am returned to court, my duty is plainly to offer my respects and allegiance to the new

Queen." His mouth tightened angrily. "I'll not be denied that right at least." Casually he dismissed the King's wrath.

"You are foolish and headstrong Tom. For your own sake I wish you would learn to accept what is already accomplished."

"It can't be left thus."

"But it must be so Tom." Alarmed by his insistence she caught at his sleeve.

"I am not afraid to risk his anger."

"Then think of me at least." Her voice grew suddenly more formal. "My Lord I am the Queen though it was not of my own choosing. But since it is done I'll not be unfaithful to my husband."

He frowned at the new note of authority in her voice. "You surely don't accept this meekly."

"My Lord what will you have me say?" She appealed to him. "Since you force me to put it more plainly, there must be no hint of those feelings we once had for each other. I can receive you only as a very dear friend, and that only with the King's full knowledge and consent."

"But Kate surely . . ."

Her hand shot up, warning him to silence. "Already you forget yourself Sir." She said it kindly but it hurt none the less. "Try to understand. My position is unsteady even now when the King's mood is good. What will happen should his anger be roused by some small incident, and you know as well as I how there are those in every court ready to intrigue and sway the King to their own advantage. My marriage does not please everyone."

"What objections can they raise Madam if the King is content?"

"Tom, the King has already rid himself of five wives. How can I be sure that my own neck is safer than the rest?

43

Every day I fear to rouse his anger however unwittingly, and even should I not do so, there are others at court only too ready to make mischief between us."

Even he had to acknowledge the truth of her words. Who indeed was to say that this sixth wife would be more fortunate than the rest. One wife more would not stir the King's conscience and Henry had ever been fickle.

"Pray God his attention will never waver then, Madam, nor his love grow less even though it means I must lose you." He said it quietly.

"Don't say it, Tom." Her lips formed the words almost soundlessly. "If I can but see you occasionally, then it must be enough. All I ask is that you understand. We must never again speak of what was once between us. For my sake and for yours."

He bowed.

"And now." She held out her hand. "I must ask you to take your leave. The King expects me in his apartments. Perhaps I can persuade him not to look too harshly upon your disobedient and foolish return to court."

His lips brushed against her fingers and then she was moving away. Her face gave no hint of the strain she was feeling.

"Goodbye, my Lord. I will put your petition to the King." Her voice returned to normality for the benefit of listening ears.

He bowed. "I congratulate the King. He has indeed found the perfect woman."

She watched, holding her head high as he left the apartment. How much better to have been that man's wife than Queen of England.

The Queen made her way hastily to the King's apartment, followed by her Ladies in Waiting. Still she could not adjust herself to the knowledge that wherever the Queen walked, so also must go that train of obedient young women, those ladies of the highest families in England who all but fought for the honour of serving at court and of waiting upon her every need.

As she moved briskly, lifting her skirts above her ankles, the sentry at the door of the King's room stepped aside, allowing her to pass. She entered the chamber, dropping a deep curtsey as her husband roared a greeting. Already her nostrils seemed to close against the stench of his person. The King waved away her ladies as Katherine rose and went forward.

"Kate, sweetheart." His hand reached out for her and she moved soundlessly to his side. "It is past the usual hour for our game with the cards. We began to think you had forgot."

She seated herself calmly beside him at the small table. "No, Your Grace. I had not forgotten." Her eyes flickered briefly away from his. It was in her mind not to mention the visit of Thomas Seymour to her apartments but caution warned that news of it would come better from her own lips than from some other who sought to make trouble. "I received a visitor, and though the hour was late I felt I should not refuse to see him."

The King smiled indulgently. "Always mindful of your duties, Kate." He leaned to kiss her cheek and she saw the grimace of pain which touched his face as he moved. "I trust it was of no consequence since it kept you from me, and not just some young man begging a few gold coins from your ever generous hands?"

Imperceptibly she hesitated, then said lightly, "It was the High Admiral."

Henry's fist tightened on the arm of his chair. His neck seemed lost between hanging layers of flesh and the rich embroidery of his shirt as his jaw thrust angrily forward. He watched her slender fingers move the cards and looked for some sign of emotion in her calm face. It filled him with fury to think she might still harbour some feelings for the man.

"This brother-of-law of mine does suddenly seem to take too much upon himself, Madam," he began irritably. "By the Lord, I gave him no leave to present himself at court. Is he so risen above himself that he thinks to overrule his King? He would be well advised to tread warily, brother or no."

Katherine's heart thudded loudly against her bodice as his face reddened with anger. She struggled to keep her hands from trembling as she studied her cards, fearing to raise his fury yet further with some unthinking word.

"I am sure only the most urgent business would have brought him to court unbidden, my Lord. Doubtless he must occasionally concern himself with the running of his estates." She smiled as she retrieved a card dropped by Henry, whose fingers seemed suddenly more clumsy than usual. "I did not think you would have me insult Queen Jane's brother by refusing to see him?"

Henry snorted, ruffling the feathers which trimmed his velvet cap. "The Admiral should be grateful he still has estates to which he may attend."

Katherine's throat tightened in an angry spasm.

"And what had he to say which was of such importance, Madam?"

"Why, no great matter, my Lord. Merely to tender his allegiance somewhat belatedly to the new Queen, which pleased me, I will confess, knowing well the regard you have for my Lord Seymour." She stressed the latter as if her husband needed to be reminded of that regard. "I was deeply touched by his words, Henry. It still comes strangely to me to hear myself acknowledged as the wife of Henry Tudor." She smiled and reached out a hand to him. "I must learn to control such pride, must I not, my Lord?"

Henry bubbled over with sudden well being. "We forgive you for such a small sin, Kate." He patted her hand and his voice seemed overly gruff as he spoke. "You will become accustomed in time to the honour."

She lowered her eyes, stifling a hysterical burst of laughter. "Perhaps for my sake you will also forgive Lord Seymour. After all, have you truly any reason to doubt the loyalty of the Seymours? Mister Parry, some wine for His Grace." She beckoned a hovering man, who filled the glass.

"Nay, he is a good man, Kate. An adventurer, a rogue with the ladies, you understand?" he warned her gently and she blushed. "But a loyal brother I will admit. I could not fail to love one of such close kin to my son. However," Henry dragged himself back to his original intent, "we think he does take advantage of that fact at times. Even Lord Seymour must learn to await our command, Kate. It will not do to let him think he can gainsay the King. He will leave court again and in good time we shall send for him."

"One might forgive him a little conceit for his joy in the King's favour, my Lord. Which any man would be proud to have. Jane's family have served you well."

Henry dropped his glass suddenly to the table, splintering the precious Venetian glass and spilling the wine, as he lowered his head to his hands with a sob of agony.

"She had no right to leave me, Kate. I needed her." Tears spilled from the sparse red lashes and Katherine knew he spoke of Jane Seymour. She felt the very real pity surge up within her breast. Typically she blamed herself for stirring up such memories and she rose swiftly, going to kneel at his side.

"You must not grieve for Jane, Your Grace." Anxiously she took his swollen hands into her own slender ones, and tried to coax him out of the depression. "She gave you your Prince and was very happy because of it. She died well content, even though her life was short. There is surely no better honour for a Queen that if she must die, it be in giving the King his heir?"

Henry sobbed, tears rolling to his cheeks as if he were some fat, over-indulged child who was denied a sweetmeat.

"Jane should have lived, Kate. Even if it meant the child had to die, but the choice was not mine. The people were entitled to their Prince."

Katherine turned her head away, sickened by the knowledge that he could so deceive himself, could find excuse for his actions even in a matter such as this. Even she knew how the King had insisted that the child be looked to first when Jane lay in torment with her labours. Such gossip travelled far from court. But she soothed him. Stroked the thinning red hair as if she believed. After all, what use was it to condemn a man to further misery; already Henry Tudor had more than enough to burden his conscience.

"I know, Henry, I know." From her sleeve she took a silk kerchief and pressed it into his hand. Pathetically he struggled to regain his self control, forcing a pitiable laugh between the tears. "Katherine Parr is poor substitute for Queen Jane, I know, but let me in turn try at least to bring you a little comfort, as is any wife's duty and pleasure to do." She looked up at him, appealing with those dark eyes,

48

and he reached down to stroke her hair, as if he would read the thoughts hidden beneath that smooth brow.

"And to think I once suspected that my High Admiral had designs upon you, Kate; to think I even feared how you might return those lustful advances."

His sharp eyes watched with innocent shrewdness. She managed to force a disbelieving laugh to her lips, and her eyes widened in surprise.

"Oh no, Henry." She heard herself say it, despising him for forcing her to yet another lie. How much had he known of Tom Seymour's hopes of marriage? The King had never liked to believe that another man could take something which he, the King, had set his heart upon. "Why, surely you could not believe it? Lord Seymour is a loyal friend, nothing more. After all, I am the King's wife, and as such he naturally gives me the respect to which such an estate entitles me, but certainly Lord Seymour cares nothing for me nor I for him, save as I would for any friend of the King's."

"So you are happy, are you, Kate?" His voice was a little sharp and she felt a shiver run along her spine.

"Who would not be happy, wed to a man such as yourself, Henry?"

He reached eagerly down, cupping her face in his hands. With surprising ferocity he kissed her full on the lips. "I am not the sweetest tempered of husbands, Kate." He made a jest of it so that she could not be sure whether it was a poor attempt at apology or excuse. "If it were not for this accursed limb I might be a merrier Monarch than I have been of late. It puts an end to my hunting, and that as you know was ever a passion of mine." He looked bitterly down at the swollen limb, remembering the days when he would have tired six horses in the chase. His mouth tightened with displeasure. "The physicians experiment with their powders and lotions. One opens the wound, another says it must be allowed to close. God's death, am I never to find ease from the torment of it?" His lips were unhealthily grey with the pain, and she marvelled at his patience. True, there were times when his rage exploded violently, but such pain would have driven a lesser man out of his senses by now.

"Will you let me tend the leg for you, Henry? After all, I have a little knowledge of such things, having nursed two husbands. I can at least try to make it a little more comfortable."

He smiled resignedly, not even daring to hope. "Do as you will, sweetheart. Though if the best doctors in England have failed, I doubt my little nurse can find any new miracle." Tolerantly he pinched her cheek and she blushed, thinking he chided her for believing herself better than his learned men.

"I can but try to ease the pain a little with my humble efforts."

Henry merely smiled and gingerly dragged himself further into the chair. With business-like haste the Queen ordered a basin of water and clean bandages to be brought. A page sped away on the errand. A wave of her hand brought Lady Margaret Neville, the step-daughter of her previous marriage, to her side.

"You will find in my apartments a soothing cream, Margaret. Take this key. You will see a small casket which contains a number of herbs and remedies. Bring the pot which has the scent of roses. My sister Lady Herbert will show you the one." The girl bustled to do her bidding, her pearl satin gown brushing heavily over the floor as she moved. The Queen then turned her attention to her own task. As she waited, she knelt beside the leg which was raised on a footstool and began to unwind those evil-smelling, pus-filled cloths. Nausea rose in her throat, yet amazingly, so real was the desire in her to lessen his pain that the feeling of horror was almost instantly dispelled.

As the wound was revealed she sat back on her heels, letting her hands rest in disbelief on the stiff folds of her gown. She looked up to his face, which had become white as chalk, and then back again to the open, running ulcer which was the size of a man's fist. Tears of pity misted her eyes.

"Oh, my dear love." It was all she could say, and the King swallowed hard, knowing for the first time in many years the true compassion of a woman who really cared.

He lay in the huge chair with his eyes closed as a page brought the things Katherine had ordered. The young man wrinkled his nose in disgust as he drew close, and seeing the gesture she waved him away with a glance of fury and a brusque lift of her hand. He retreated shamefacedly, admiring the Queen greatly for her lack of fear in the task she undertook.

Gently she bathed away the pus and blood until the wound seemed clean. She could only imagine what effort it must cost the King to remain motionless as she worked. Her fingers gently applied the soothing cream which Margaret Neville held for her, and then a soft bandage covered the ulcer. When it was done she looked up again at her husband, afraid that it must have been almost more than he could bear, but to her amazement he sat watching her with such an expression upon his face that she could only remain silent.

"Kate." Gently he said her name and she moved instinctively closer. His hands urged her up from her knees and she eased herself painfully from her position to sit at his side. Tenderly he brushed his lips against her brow, caressing the dark hair which escaped from beneath the jewelled hood. In that moment she saw the King as no other had ever seen him. As a man full of gentleness and of love. A man who was sick and grew old, looking desperately for comfort, and in that instant she resolved to be that comfort. Her mouth responded for the first time to the kiss he pressed almost reluctantly on to her lips. They broke apart a full minute later, both tasting the salt of tears in their mouths.

"My sweet, gentle little nurse." He sighed the words. "If I had only known you all those years ago my life would have been vastly different. Why have you come to me now when it is too late?"

"You have me now and for as long as you need me, Your Grace." She tried to reassure him. "It is not too late; don't even think it."

"I shall always need you, Kate." His face crumpled with misery again. "Don't ever let them take you from me too."

"No one shall take me from my husband, unless it be your wish. Rest easy now," she soothed. "The leg will give you no more pain this night. I give you my word on it. I shall stay here beside you."

He rested his head back against the chair and realised that she spoke the truth. For the first time in many months the unspeakable agony was gone. He could close his eyes and really sleep and his sweetheart was there at his side ready to ease his agony whenever he asked it.

What wisdom had led him to wed the Lady Katherine? Nothing would induce him to part with his gentle nurse. The King drifted into an easy sleep, his hand still clasping tightly the Queen's fingers as if he was afraid to lose her.

FIVE

By CHRISTMAS, the King's condition was so much alleviated that for the first time in many years the court celebrated the holiday with great joy.

Queen Katherine watched closely for any sign of pain in his grey eyes, and when the strain of the occasion began to show in his face she would find some excuse to bring the festivities to an early close. Her influence was such that no member of the court thought to question her quiet authority now. Queen Katherine's word was as well respected as the King's. Henry made no protest, though realising that her pleas of a headache or weariness were but a means of persuading him to retire, yet what might once have thrown the great Tudor into a terrible fury, he now accepted meekly, realising that it was merely a measure of her love for him. Such was the influence of Katherine Parr upon the Monarch.

For the most part the court welcomed this new docility in the once fiery-tempered King, and gave the Queen her due respect, recognising the power she now held. Yet with some, caution warned that she must still tread warily, for though they offered her respect as the King's wife, never was there the tolerance and support she had hoped for. Her shrewd eyes gave no hint of this knowledge. It was sufficient for the gentle lady to have their obedience, time enough to win their approval.

After six months of marriage the King seemed still well

content with his bride. It was perhaps too much to hope that some ambitious fellow would not seek to alter that happy state by finding some fault which could be used as a lever to weaken her ties with Henry VIIIth.

With the new year the Queen hoped to persuade the King to allow her to bring the royal children to Hampton Court.

"I see so little of Edward and the Princesses, my love," she explained, "and it grieves me. They are, after all, your own children, my step-children, and I would care for them as my own."

She sat on a stool with her green velvet gown spread about her, tending as always the King's leg. It was a task which the Sovereign allowed only his wife to undertake these days, for no other could bring such relief, and none argued with the King. It was a burden they handed over gratefully to the new Queen.

"Have you not sufficient duties, Kate, that you must look for more?" Henry teased her playfully, and she smiled, pleased to see him in such good humour.

"I feel that the Queen should in some measure be responsible for the welfare and education of the royal children, Henry. Edward is now six. It is time his Latin and French studies were taken seriously. In any event, it would not be a duty but a pleasure. Edward is a sweet child."

"And we cannot have the world say that England's heir is an ignoramus, eh, sweetheart?" He twitched a finger at her nose and she flushed a little.

"I did not mean it so, Henry." Her dark head was lowered so that he saw only the top of her green hood and the rows of pearls stitched on to it. "You have three admirable children; 'tis just that I long to have children about me. I would be a true mother to the Prince and Princesses."

The King's face saddened a little, and he frowned, pressing his fingertips together.

"I had hoped there might be some sign of a babe of our own by now, Kate."

Warily she glanced up at him; her heart beat rapidly. "I did warn you before we were wed, my lord, that I had never had any hopes of a child by my previous husbands. It did not seem to worry you then."

"Nor does it now, sweetheart." He answered perhaps a shade too quickly. "And, after all, 'tis early days yet."

Katherine looked away. He was surely not going to taunt her with her barren state? It had seemed not to matter until now. Was this perhaps the first tiny warning that she must tread carefully?

"Will you permit me to bring the children to court, Henry?" She insisted to divert him again to the original argument and away from this suddenly dangerous ground. "Mary and I are of similar age. She would be excellent company for me. And Elizabeth, well, my lord, she is at an age when she needs a mother's guidance."

His lips pursed tightly at this mention of his red haired child. There was in the younger princess a strong spirit of rebellion. A fiery temper which he recognised as being too closely akin to his own. It was something which should have drawn them closer, but he could never forgive the girl for being Anne Boleyn's child. The courts had tried to accuse Anne at her trial of incest, saying that the red haired babe was her brother's child and not the King's. His face darkened vividly as he recalled how willingly he had allowed himself to be persuaded. Yet never could he truly believe the babe was not his, when every movement, every gesture, was an echo of himself.

55

Katherine watched his expression anxiously, almost wishing she had not broached this delicate subject, yet the welfare of her step-children concerned her greatly and she was not prepared to be denied in this issue.

"The Princess Elizabeth and I seem to strike sparks whenever we meet," Henry said with some anger. "We are not sure it would be wise to have her at court, sweetheart."

"But what is more natural than a few sparks when two such vigorous, red haired rebels meet, my love?" Katherine Parr laughed despite his frown of displeasure. "She has your own spirit of fair play, your own fierce determination. Where is the wrong in it? It has, after all, made you the best loved King in Christendom."

His mouth curved into a reluctant smile.

"I am persuaded, Kate, that you will always outwit me in any argument. You defeat me every time, and I am not sure it pleases me." He pretended mock anger with her and she looked away, trying not to laugh.

"Your Grace is really not trying. I declare when you set your mind to it even the most knowledgeable courtier must retire a feeble loser against your keen wit. 'Tis just that your heart is not in this argument, and I can scarce claim to be more than a feeble-witted woman, so that if I seem to differ from the views of my King, it is not sharp wits but more womanly instinct which leads me to press selfishly for the comfort of these children."

He eyed her shrewdly. "There is nothing feeble witted in you, Kate." His hand gripped hers tightly. "You know what you are about, but it pleases me to give in to your demands, which are ever reasonable and unselfish."

"Then you will have the children brought to court?" Her face lit with pleasure.

"Do as you will, sweetheart, if it pleases you." He always loved to seem generous.

The Queen was already on her feet. Her lips brushed against his cap. "I will go this very moment with your permission, and send messages to them."

"You are a witch, Kate. You twist me round those shapely fingers of yours so that I can refuse you nothing." He watched as she made her curtsey and then flew to the door, her mind already with the Prince and Princesses.

He could not even find it in his heart to blame her for their lack of heirs. After all, they had only been wed these six months. There was still time. For the present let her amuse herself with the children of his past wives if it pleased her. He had already given discreet orders that the royal nursery should always be kept in readiness for yet another Prince.

The Princess Mary was seated at a writing desk beside the Queen her step-mother. Their two dark heads were bent over the books, Mary's unadorned gown of dark blue crushed against the folds of rose and gold which fell from Katherine's slightly taller figure.

"The translation goes well, Mary. I am exceedingly pleased with it." The Queen smiled her pleasure and the Princess's plain face flushed brilliantly. She was not accustomed to receiving praise.

"I could not have done it without your help, Madam," she replied modestly.

"Oh, nonsense. Your Latin is of the best and this was not the easiest of works."

Mary rose from the desk and stood watching the Queen. Idly she traced a finger over the carved woodwork of a chair. "I cannot think why I allowed myself to be persuaded to undertake the translation, Madam. You know well that my views in the matter of religion are vastly opposed to your own." Her brown eyes faced her stepmother honestly.

Katherine studied her seriously for a moment and she laid aside the quill.

"You feel you betray your Catholic faith simply because I ask you to translate from the Latin the works of the Gospels? Why, my almoner, Master Miles Coverdale, finds your work exceptionally good and you did not make complaint of the task, Mary."

Mary's gaze fell. "You are Queen, Madam. It is not for me to argue." She clasped her fingers nervously, seeming almost a child rather than a grown woman. Katherine went to her and put her hands upon the thin shoulders as she looked into her step-daughter's eyes.

"Mary, you know I would not compel you to anything, but can you not admit that you see the wisdom of translating these works into English so that your fellow countrymen may read for themselves? Why should such words be available only to the few who can read Latin? Should not every man be able to judge for himself what is true? Surely it was for this reason that you undertook the work?"

The Princess moved away from the Queen's searching gaze. "What troubles me, Madam, is that you should look to encourage the people towards the Reformed Religion. It is most unwise in you to make your views known when the King's loyalty is pledged to the Catholic Church in England. My father may look with some tolerance upon your actions, but there are others who will be only too eager to use this as a means of turning the King from you. Be warned, Madam," she appealed. "My father has wed six times, and always there are factions prepared to further

58

their own cause, whatever the cost. Your Protestant followers are few. You cannot hope to win. Certainly you cannot hope to convert all England and still think to keep your head upon your shoulders."

Katherine's face whitened.

"I did not realise my views were so well known. I have not knowingly thrust them upon any person."

"You would not have to, Madam. There are those who watch and wait. They call themselves the King's men, but Catholic though I am I do not approve necessarily of their methods. I undertake this work for you in the privacy of these apartments, yet I'll wager there are those who know of it and will use the knowledge when it suits their purpose."

Katherine's brow furrowed beneath her hood.

"You think the King would heed such malicious talk against me? He seems well content with our marriage, Mary."

The Princess shrugged unhappily.

"They know how to work upon his moods and I have reason enough to know it. I have too great a fondness for you to see you fall victim to their plotting, which is why I warn you. I will readily work on the translation for you since it gives you pleasure, and I take no offence in the work but some will grasp eagerly at it, as but the first means to bring about ill feeling between yourself and the King."

The Queen nodded miserably and moved to the window.

"I made the mistake of allowing myself to become overconfident. Yet I was so sure of the King's love for me."

"He does love you, Madam. Even I can see it, but who knows how quickly he will tire, want some other diversion? Can you not see, Madam, how the council pander to these moods, these whims, when it seems he must convince himself again of his manhood by chasing some new woman? The council will be only too grateful for the opportunity to replace you with a true Catholic, someone who will sway the King to their own way of thinking."

"But of whom should I beware, Mary? How can I know . . . ?"

"Have you not your suspicions, Madam? You must surely have learned by now with whom you may speak freely and whom you must treat with caution."

Katherine stared unseeing out of the window. "The very fact that I am the King's wife means that I am always surrounded by men and women looking to further their own ends. There are so many. How can I tell who is my friend?"

Mary bit her lip. It was not for her to name names. The Queen had been warned; let her now look to her own safety. Much as she loved this new step-mother, her Papist heart would never see things through the Queen's eyes.

"I can only warn you to be on your guard, Madam. I'll not interfere in any business concerning the King my father. I have learned to my cost over the years to keep silent on the matter of religion. I cannot afford to give any faction cause to say I uphold their views. My thoughts are my own."

The Queen understood and smiled a little wearily at her step-daughter.

"I thank you for the warning, Mary. I must try to ensure that no action of mine stirs the King to anger, though I'll not deny my religion to do it."

"It may not be necessary, Madam, so long as the King is given no excuse to look for faults in you."

Katherine nodded and changed the subject, for it depressed her suddenly.

"Shall we go to your brother's apartments and see how he progresses with his Latin? The King will be pleased to hear a good report of his son."

Mary smiled indulgently. "I think Edward's thoughts are more occupied with the King's Men at Arms, Madam, since he returned to court, than with his studies. At Hunsden he was strictly tutored. So much so, in fact, that I fear his strength was overtaxed. He looks very pale."

The Queen agreed with this latter, frowning a little. "His cough is too persistent, I agree, and the King has also spoken of it." She smiled indulgently. "I think your father will not begrudge Edward a lapse from studies, but we must look to it that the Prince does not altogether forget his duties. After all, the Heir Presumptive cannot be allowed to grow up an idiot."

Mary's cheeks flushed a little. Once long ago she had been recognised as the heir to her father's crown, in those days before the coming of Nan Bullen. It had been bitter gall to the small Princess to find herself set aside for the baby Elizabeth. Even now when the two Princesses were older, the resentment still remained, though with the birth of Edward to Queen Jane Seymour both had been set aside yet again in the succession. With the King's sixth marriage Henry had declared that any children he should have by Queen Katherine would also take precedence over his two daughters, so it seemed more unlikely with each year that either Mary or Elizabeth would ever achieve that elusive crown of England.

Katherine watched the flicker of depression in Mary's eyes and her heart bled for the woman, who, though almost her own age, had never been wed. The King had been guilty of many sins, yet by far the worst was this, that he should have dashed any hopes of a marriage for his daughter by labelling her bastard before the world. No Royal House in Europe would make an alliance with a Princess who had naught but a name.

She put her hands gently about Mary's shoulders and deliberately chose to misunderstand the scowl which was set on those thin features.

"You must not worry about Edward, my dear. The King's physicians assure us that he will outgrow the weakness. Many children suffer these little ailments and yet grow up to be healthy and none the worse for them."

Mary shook off her mood. She genuinely loved her infant brother and could never honestly begrudge him that crown.

"I pray God they are correct, Madam. He is far too thin for his age."

"Shall we go and see for ourselves whether he studies or plays, Mary? Perhaps we might persuade his tutor to release him just for one hour so that we can walk in the gardens." Persuasively she moved with the Princess to the door. Their gowns brushed gently together. They might almost have been sisters, and both were drawn closer still by the man who held within his temperamental hands their very existence.

SIX

MY LORD GARDINER, Bishop of Winchester, bowed formally before his Sovereign. His sharp eyes noted immediately the sullen droop to the King's mouth, the slight purpling of the gross face. Not many would have sought audience with His Grace knowing that the royal leg was particularly painful today, and that the royal temper was therefore very much roused. But it suited Gardiner's purpose very well. His colourless eyes were expressionless as he waited.

"Well, what is it, Gardiner?" Henry winced and eased his leg with ham-like fists further on to the foot-stool. He bit his lip to prevent a further gasp of pain. He was in no mood to listen to complaining Bishops.

Gardiner shuffled forward, apparently oblivious to his Monarch's discomfort.

"I have spoken briefly before of the concern within the Church of the gradual increase in favour towards the Reformed Religion, Your Grace." He saw from beneath his thin lashes the frown of displeasure which greeted his words, but was not put off by it. "It is becoming too great a threat to be ignored, Your Grace," he persisted. "Since you broke away from Rome and pronounced yourself Head of the Catholic Church in England, the people naturally look to you to settle these disputes and put down the rebels before they become too great a danger. Something must be done, Sire, before it is too late."

Henry bit back a violent oath. He was no feeble wit that he could not see what Gardiner was about. There had been many such subtle hints from the man against the Queen, but until now the King had chosen to ignore them. It mattered little to him what Katherine's beliefs were, so long as she caused no outright rebellion against himself, but the Bishop's constant references to her 'unfortunate leanings' were beginning to irritate.

"What is it you would have me do, Bishop?" he questioned irritably. "You talk of 'the rebels', the 'anti-Papists', yet never mention names, never give me proof. God's death, man, do you expect me to act against shadows? Show me some proof of treason and I will consider it further." He sank back into the chair, puffing with anger and pain. "But one thing more, my Lord Bishop, be warned . . ." His eyes narrowed. "Don't meddle in matters which are my own concern. It would make me very angry to hear aught said of those close to me. You understand me, Gardiner?" He leaned forward insistently, his arms clasping the great carved sides of his chair.

Gardiner understood only too well. His mouth felt suddenly dry. Henry Tudor was still so besotted with his bride that he would hear no ill against her, not even treason.

The King's hand strayed unconsciously to the leg as a hot knife seemed to twist within the open wound. For a second his eyes closed and the Bishop wondered whether the Queen's hold was perhaps as great as he, and indeed, the King, imagined. It was true that Katherine Parr's fingers could ease the pain, but might it also be that this was the strongest, perhaps the only, real tie which bound her to her fickle husband? If evidence could be found or manufactured, and a slow but unceasing campaign of discrediting factors aimed at the Queen, in time the King might be persuaded to look elsewhere for his comfort.

"I will find that proof and Your Grace shall judge whether there is treason or not. Your Council only seek to protect you from the plotting of malcontents, Sire. We want only to save you from further misery." His thin face was sharp, almost ratlike, as he stood clasping his hands together, making repetitive half bows and reassuring noises.

The King sighed and nodded wearily. In the past he might have been aroused to take action, but now all he longed for was Kate. To have her gentle fingers bathe the wound and ease his agony.

"I'll not argue with your motives, Bishop. I dare say your intentions are good, but I must have more than words."

The Bishop became eager and he drew closer to the raised dais. "We must make a thorough search of the town, Your Grace. The people will resent it, of course, so that we must have an official order signed by your own hand, but there are books, papers, all manner of evidence if only we can gather it."

Henry longed only to be rid of this persistent tormentor. "Search where you will, Gardiner; only spare me the details, I beg you."

"No place shall be exempt, Your Grace. Every stone will be turned." He was already retreating backwards towards the door.

"One moment." Henry's voice halted his progress and he paused, knowing a sudden almost sickening disappointment. "You may search any house within the town as you see fit, but the Palace you will not disturb. Do you understand me, my Lord? The apartments of the Queen are as private as my own and will not be looked into. As your better, the Queen may rightly expect to retain her privacy and will not be subjected to the indignity of such a search." He smiled and waved a hand. "You may go, Bishop, and I shall look to hear news of your venture as soon as it is accomplished."

Gardiner cursed silently, controlling his features as he withdrew. His lips compressed tightly. So once again he was to be cheated of victory. He was certain the Queen's apartments would yield a rich haul of evidence. Like a nervous rabbit he scuttled along the corridor, hugging his robes about him.

"Well, no matter, Madam. This time you escape, but there is more than one way to uncrown a Queen."

As he proceeded past the Queen's apartments and on to his small room in a far wing of the Palace, he encountered the Lady Anne Herbert, sister of Queen Katherine. She was accompanied by another young woman. For a second he hesitated, his brow wrinkling as he tried to recall a name. Aye, it was Mistress Anne Askew.

It was this latter who caused the Bishop to falter in his step and stare openly at the two as they made their way to the royal apartments. He knew little of that lady, save that she had been turned out of her home by her husband and was denied by the rest of her family for daring to confess her belief in the Reformed Faith. This was not the first time he had seen the Lady about the Palace; in fact, she was now a constant visitor, welcomed by the Queen, who pitied the girl for her misfortunes. This snippet of unexpected intelligence afforded the Bishop a swift return to good humour and he went on his way with a lighter step. It was something he must dwell on further, this connection of the Queen with a known heretic.

Anne Askew frowned but said nothing as the man's sharp eyes dwelt on her with considerable intensity. Her companion, Lady Herbert, appeared to have noticed nothing and as they had now reached the Queen's apartment the matter was temporarily forgotten.

The two women entered making their curtseys, and Katherine greeted them with a cry of pleasure. She kissed her sister warmly and then embraced the other woman fondly.

"Anne, it is good to see you again." But her eyes flickered severely over her friend. "You are thin, Mistress, much too thin. And so pale." She held the young woman at arm's length, studying the fair features critically. "What brings this change in you since we last met?"

Anne Askew smiled, showing her white, even teeth. "Your Grace has sharp eyes, but it is nothing."

"Nothing?" Lady Herbert broke in sharply. "How can you say it is nothing to be persecuted for your beliefs?" She looked to her sister appealingly for help. "Her husband, Mister Kyme, casts her out of the house because her beliefs do not conform to his own. She has neither money, save what her friends can provide, and no means of protection against the men who threaten her in the King's name. Dear Lord, is it any wonder she looks so ill? To be called heretic and either scorned or feared by everyone she mets. To be in constant dread for one's life—that were enough to make anyone ill, Madam."

The Queen's eyes widened in disbelief.

"Anne, is this true? Are you indeed so persecuted?"

The girl lifted her shoulders with a wry smile. "We are all learning what it is to defy the King's advisers, Madam?"

"But who?" Katherine cried. "Who does this in the King's name? Believe me, Anne, this is not the King's work, for he knows well enough of my own beliefs and has never made complaint of them. Why, we have had many friendly arguments upon the subject of religion. He would not do this, Anne."

Lady Herbert pushed a chair close to the Queen and sat, spreading her yellow gown about her.

"The King may look with tolerance upon his wife's actions, Madam, but it does not mean he condones rebellion in his other subjects." She fingered a medallion which hung about her neck and frowned. "Katherine, I must say this. Should you not have a care for your own safety? It becomes widely known now that the Queen's household have discussions upon the Reformed Faith, and we have all begun to notice a certain extra observation. Our movements are watched. Have you not seen it?"

The Queen stared at her sister, scarcely understanding.

"One inevitably expects the curious glances when one is raised so suddenly to be a Queen. But is it possible I could have mistaken them?"

"On our way to your rooms we passed Bishop Gardiner. His expression, Madam, was most revealing. He was never a friend to the Protestants and he spends a great deal of time with the King of late." Anne Askew laid a book she had been carrying on the Queen's table. "He saw this, Madam; possibly its significance will escape him, though I doubt it. His eyes are sharp; you should beware that he doesn't see too much of your own business. It will achieve nothing to openly give him reason to name you traitor. The King would not forgive even you such a charge. Indeed, could not forgive it if the Bishop manages to rouse the people against you, and it has been done before, Madam."

Katherine took the book quickly and laid it amongst the papers in her desk. She locked it and secured the key on a chain which hung from her waist.

"It seems I have been blind, ladies. Perhaps we are all undone by my foolishness."

Anne Herbert shook her head. "The blame rests with no one person, but we must all have more care. Anne is denied her husband's name and his house. The persecution begins in a small way with those close to the Queen." She spread her fingers despairingly. "Who can say how long it will be before they dare to accuse the Queen herself?"

"It has been done too many times before, Madam," Anne Askew reminded the white-faced Queen. "Queen Anne Boleyn went to the block, condemned by charges which many could never believe. Catherine of Aragon also suffered at the hands of the King's men for her beliefs. You must watch and tread warily. Never give the King reason to become angry with you or 'tis the first step taken towards certain death."

The Queen gathered up the folds of her blue velvet gown and walked slowly to the large hearth where a fire blazed. Her ladies were busily occupied with the embroidering of cloths for the Church and could hear no word which passed between the Queen and her companions.

"Perhaps I should speak with the King of my feelings upon this growing persecution. I hadn't realised until now just how greatly my beliefs have offended." Katherine stared into the flames dejectedly.

Lady Herbert shot her a glance of pity.

"I will say this, Madam, because you are my sister as well as my Queen. The King prefers to have an easy conscience. You know it, we all know it. If you go to him with this, he will be involved, however unwillingly. He will be forced to take sides with one party or another and we can none of us afford to take the risk. Though he loves his wife, his duty to the country is greater. Never ask him to make such a choice, sister, for you would be the certain loser."

The Queen looked from her sister to young Anne Askew.

"But there must surely be something I can do. I can't sit idly by and watch my friends suffer, whilst I remain untouched because I am the King's wife. Were it not for my encouragement none of this would have happened."

"That is not true, Madam," Anne Askew interrupted kindly. "It is true that your own interest in the faith has encouraged us to speak more openly, but even before you came the feeling was strong among us."

"That makes my conscience no easier, Anne. I should

have given thought to the safety of others before encouraging such talk."

"It would have happened sooner or later, Madam—this questioning of the Catholic views. If not now, then five years from now, ten years . . . who can say? All we can do is to be sure that no evidence can be found for Gardiner and his colleagues to work on. It were perhaps better if I left, Madam. Already the Bishop has noted my visits to your apartment and will draw his own assumptions from it."

Katherine held out her hands. Tears glistened on her dark lashes as she embraced the woman. "Then I thank you for coming to me, Anne, for sharing some of that faith and strength with me. But look to yourself and don't worry for my danger. I shall be quite safe."

Anne shook her head regretfully.

"I wish I could be sure of it, Madam. It would strike a terrible blow to our cause should you come to harm because of it."

"I shall watch, Anne, don't fear. I think I understand the King's humours well enough to be able to protect myself. Go now and do what you have to do. There are some I must also warn. Pray God we are not already too late. Who can tell how far the Bishop has already wormed his way into the King's mind?"

Anne Askew made a solemn curtsey, sweeping back the heavy crimson brocade of her skirts; then silently she withdrew, leaving the Queen to consider how best she might protect her friends and also her own already shaking security.

SEVEN

"Madam." Lady Herbert's voice cracked hoarsely in the small apartment as she made a hurried entrance, almost flinging herself forward in her effort to reach the Queen. Visibly she swayed and, seeing the terror written upon the chalk-white face, Katherine sped instantly forward to support the woman flinging aside the embroidery at which she worked.

"Merciful heavens what is it sister? You look as if you had seen a ghost. Lady Tyrwhitt bring some wine quickly." She took the glass from a woman who hurried forward and pressed it insistently into the trembling hands. "Now drink this and try to calm yourself." Patiently she stood as Lady Herbert gulped the wine between sobs of terror, spilling drops of the red liquid onto her pale green gown. Katherine took the glass swiftly.

"Forgive me Madam." Lady Herbert's hands clutched frantically at a small lace kerchief which she dabbed ineffectively at the staining, yet her hands trembled so fiercely that the Queen knew she moved automatically and was not truly aware of any action she made.

Katherine knelt suddenly beside the chair, taking the young woman's shaking hands into her own.

"Now tell me, slowly and plainly what it is that throws you into such a stir. No, look at me." She commanded with kindly severity. She turned Anne's face to her own. "I cannot help unless you tell me."

Lady Herbert blinked miserably at her through a mist of tears. "It is too late for any to speak of help now Madam." Desolately she lowered her head unable to brush away the flowing tears since her hands were still held firmly.

"Why did none of us see the danger?"

The Queen reached for a stool and sat beside the woman. "Now speak more coherently sister. I am trying to understand, but thus far you have told me nothing. If you are in some danger then tell me and we shall see if something cannot be done to divert it."

"Madam we are all in sore need of help. Have you not heard? Anne Askew has been arrested by the King's men and put to the torture."

Katherine rose unsteadily from the stool. Blankly she stared down at her kinswoman. "You are surely misinformed."

"Nay Madam. I wish it were so. When the news reached me I also refused to believe it, but the source of the information is reliable. A young woman of my own household, a follower of the New Religion like ourselves was speaking with a member of the Tower guard. At first she paid him no real mind but when Mistress Askew's name was mentioned she became more alert and gleaned this dreadful information without raising any suspicion."

"But in the Lord's name why?" The Queen responded vehemently. "What has Anne Askew done to merit such villainous treatment? And why such secrecy?"

"As to that I can only guess. Remember we had ample warning of Gardiner's interference. He will do his utmost to cause a breach between yourself and the King and what better way to do it than this? If he can but prove that Anne Askew gives ear to the New Religion, and that the lady is received warmly into the Queen's circle of close friends and confidantes, will not the King draw his own conclusions? Even should His Grace fail to do so, then there will be someone swift enough to do so for him."

"But if as you say the King gives ear so readily to the Bishop, then why has he not reproached me for my interest in the New Learning and expressed his displeasure of it?" Katherine fingered the black and gold brocade of her sleeve nervously.

"Perhaps the King loves you too well Madam, but discontent can eat gradually into the mind. Men such as Gardiner work slowly but methodically and by choosing their moment can force the King's hand. If it can be proved that you openly welcome the New Faith and encourage it in direct opposition to your husband's wishes, then they will call it treason and the King is presented with a *fait accompli*. After all how can he forgive in the Queen what another subject may be put to death for?"

"Put to death?" The words were forced from dry lips.

Lady Herbert looked at her in some surprise. "The questioners do their work well, there is evidence enough of that over the past years. Obviously subtle methods have failed to produce the answers required from Mistress Askew and it was necessary to use more forceful methods. My servant discovered this much at least and took some risk in doing it."

"But the lady has never made any secret of her beliefs, on the contrary she declares them openly. Why then should they use her so harshly now?"

Lady Herbert sprang to face her sister angrily pushing aside the restricting folds of heavy green brocade which whirled about her ankles.

"God's death Madam there is surely only one answer

to that. They try to force her to name the Queen as her accomplice and when she would not, Gardiner and Lord Chancellor Wriothesly gave the order for her to be put upon the rack. The young man of the Tower guard boasted openly of it, that at first Mister Knevet the Lord Lieutenant thought to frighten her into submission merely by showing her the foul instrument of torture used in that Godforsaken place, but when she still remained firm my Lord Wriothesly gave up all pretence and did himself inflict the punishment, putting his own hand to the rack."

Katherine turned away feeling suddenly sickened. She pressed a hand to her mouth and leaned against the desk for support. "She should have given the name they required."

"It would not have saved her Madam. Mistress Askew is but a small pawn in this business. Every blow struck at the Reformed Religion adds to Gardiner's pleasure and Anne was always a strong opponent. The Bishop knows well of your own views but he has to find some way of forcing the King's hand."

"I must go to the King." Already Katherine was gathering up her gown and speeding towards the door but Lady Herbert ran after her, frantically clutching at her sleeve.

"Sister, no." Insistently she tugged, restraining the Queen driven on to such indiscretion by fear. "Will you give them the opportunity to put your head on the block? What can you hope to achieve?"

Katherine's pale face looked despairingly down at her sister.

"I am not sure yet what I can achieve, but one thing is clear I cannot simply sit by and watch my friends tortured and persecuted when it is my own neck they really want. Gardiner will be content with my life, though

74

Dear God why any man should see reason for offence in my reading Tyndale's translation of the New Testament I am at a loss to understand."

"You know as well as I that there is more to it Madam. Bishop Gardiner is afraid of losing the King's favour. Slowly over these past eight years he has urged your husband back towards the Catholic faith. True the King will never look to Rome again, will always style himself Supreme Head of the Church in England, but it is sufficient for Gardiner and others like him to have the King consent to the Statute of the Six Articles."

Katherine laughed scornfully. "And it was well renamed the 'Bloody Statute'. What right has any man to prevent the reading of the English Bible or the many scholarly works on the subject of religion? Why should a priest be denied the right to marry and what purpose can it possibly serve to compel people to attend the Mass? All I ask is the right to question. The right to argue. It is all Anne Askew wanted and Dear God I shall ask the King why she is denied that right."

"He will make you no answer unless it be to order your arrest for treason Madam. The King is a sick man, grown too weary to listen to squabbling courtiers."

"But if I stand by without making some effort, how many more of my dearest friends must suffer simply because Gardiner is afraid of my influence with the King?" Her brow creased in bewilderment. "Henry is fond of me, yet I often ask myself of late how greatly that fondness is influenced by my skills as a nurse."

"Then I beg you not to seek to find the answer by forcing him to take sides Madam."

"But Anne I must. Surely you can see it of all people?"

Lady Herbert shrugged despondently. "If anything were

75

to happen to you, it would set back the Reformation by a decade at least. The people begin to take heart because of your interest. They begin to want the services to be read slowly in English so that they may understand and question, and with your help, your influence with the King it seemed for a while that it might become the rule. Don't undo it all Katherine. Don't deny them your support now, simply be less fervent for a while in your opinions."

"I deny them nothing Anne." The Queen cried. "It is for their sakes that I go to the King."

"But he will not heed you Madam, not so long as Gardiner is there to whisper in his ear causing trouble."

Katherine turned angrily away with a sigh. She looked up at the ceiling as if hoping for some inspiration. "I wished the Bishop no harm 'til now. Far from it, I would have welcomed him as my friend. But since he has chosen to become my enemy I must at least prepare some defence against him. I can't stand by and see him poison the King's mind against me." She clasped her hands together tightly so that the knuckles showed white. Her wide turned back sleeves fell heavily against her gown, revealing the false, embroidered puffing of another sleeve beneath.

"I think you make a grave error in going to the King, Madam." Anne Herbert shook her head sadly. "But I'll not urge you any further, I can see it would be useless."

Katherine took the girl's hand swiftly in her own. "Anne I am no fool. The King was no starry-eyed youth when he wed me. It was not a match conceived of great passion yet something holds us together. I can't believe the King will readily listen to gossip against me, he seems too well content to have things as they are."

Lady Herbert clasped her hands in her lap as she

76

watched her sister's torment. From a stool, her anxious face watched the Queen's fretful pacing.

"Whatever his motives in marrying you. I will admit the King seems well pleased with his sixth wife now. This marriage has brought him more peace than any of the others at least."

"But for how long will that peace last if Gardiner manages to destroy it? If there is nothing stronger than my skills as a nurse to hold me to the King am I then to be removed as cleverly as the rest?" Her hand beat against the table in furious resentment. "I am not only feared for my own life Anne. What of the rest of my family, what of you? Have you realised yet that if the Queen falls then so do you, and Margaret Neville and any other member of my unfortunate family?"

Anne Herbert's mouth trembled a little and then her head lifted defiantly.

"I am not afraid for myself sister. Henry Tudor chose you to be his wife, to comfort him in old age and sickness. You know him better than most."

"And thank God I can at least give him that comfort Anne. But old and sick as he is, with such men as the Bishop to meddle he may be won from me yet. Which is why I have no choice but to go to him and plead my cause. Who knows what other lies they may use against me? Far better to discover now than remain silent and learn the full extent of their malice when it is too late."

"Lies can do you no harm if they are without foundation, and no person can point the finger at your past which has been blameless."

Katherine nodded uncertainly. "But where evidence may not be found, it can be manufactured Anne. There are times of late when I scarce dare to speak at all lest someone report every word to the Bishop and his followers. For my own peace of mind I must speak with the King and see how matters lie. Anne Askew is the first. If I can prevent it there shall be no more good lives threatened because of my own beliefs." She hesitated. "A word of warning Anne, if you have any books of mine concerned with the New Learning, or indeed any literature of that nature then keep them well hidden or burn them. So far the Palace is safe but not for much longer I think."

The young woman nodded and rose from the stool, automatically smoothing down the folds of her gown. "God go with you then Katherine since you are determined. I argue not with your reasons but with the wisdom of facing the King."

Katherine embraced the girl fondly and smiled as Anne Herbert curtsied before withdrawing. Her mind was already seeking the words for her appeal to the weary Monarch.

EIGHT

"YOUR GRACE." Katherine knelt humbly before her husband, her gaze flickering warily as she lifted her head towards the King and the man who stood at his side. To her dismay she recognised the very cause of her fears, Gardiner, Bishop of Winchester.

"Rise Madam." Henry's voice beckoned her forward without its usual warmth and she stood hesitantly, meeting the full force of those small, pig-like eyes and wondering why her knees should suddenly tremble so. Beneath her lashes she cast a glance at Gardiner and saw the malicious hint of triumph which played about the cruel lips. He returned the furtive look without blinking and she felt even more discomfited by his presence.

Straightening and lifting her head she went to the King's side carefully avoiding the leg which was raised on a foot-stool.

"My apologies for this intrusion Sire, I had not thought to find you occupied." She addressed him formally since he made no move to welcome her with customary familiarity.

His small mouth pursed angrily, seeming ridiculously out of place in so large a face.

"We have never yet allowed ill health to interfere with our duties Madam. I am as yet still King in this realm and will not be accused of neglecting any matter."

Such temper she had become accustomed to whenever the leg troubled him and she reached out gently with her hand. "Shall I tend the leg for Your Grace?" As always concerned despite her fears for his comfort.

For a moment it seemed he was almost about to welcome her ministering hands on the burning sore, when Gardiner coughed lightly and he bit back the words, remembering instead the other business which the Bishop had brought to his attention.

"Nay leave it Madam." He brushed her away resent-fully. "You seek as always to interpret our wish before it is spoken. You meddle too much Katherine methinks, in matters which do not concern you."

Her heart lurched sickeningly at this unfair abuse. She longed to face Gardiner with her accusations, realising well enough where this antagonism had started but she kept her gaze firmly fixed on Henry.

"Your Grace if I seem to interest myself overmuch in the

affairs of this court, 'tis only because I am concerned always for your contentment and peace of mind. When you made me Queen I believed this to be one of the many duties required of me, and one I undertook willingly, having so great a love of my husband and King."

His lips twitched in a momentary spasm of guilt and love as he studied her pale face. He did not doubt for one moment that she spoke the truth. Kate did not lie, yet he couldn't dismiss the Bishop's warnings lightly. He must make her see that she dabbled unwisely in some things.

"As my Queen you are vulnerable Madam, and should remember it. I raised you to be first lady in this land, but like any wife your obedience must first and foremost be to the King your husband. The people look to you for example. How think you they will construe it when the Queen herself flouts our wishes?" His narrowed eyes watched closely as she bit nervously at her lower lip, and it pained him more than a little to know that Kate was undoubtedly no more than an innocent victim of politicians as he was.

"Your Grace I offer no disobedience." Her slender hand gestured appealingly towards him as if expecting help. "All I ask is the right to question and study the works of certain scholars . . ."

"It is not for you to question Madam." Henry leaned suddenly forward, his pink face drawing closer to her own. "Women have other duties, occupy yourself with your needlework and the getting of my babes. This is woman's work. Leave the rest to men."

Katherine flinched at the venomous reminder that as yet she had failed to conceive the child he still dreamed of. Dumbly she lowered her head, fighting back the tears. She longed to escape his anger and the contempt of Gardiner whose eyes seemed to bore down on to the back of her hood. But there was still something which must be done . . .

"Your Grace . . ." She faltered and looked up into her husband's face. "I came here to beg your mercy. Not for myself but for a young woman who has committed no sin, yet suffers foul torture at the hands of men accomplished in such things."

"We do not torture women Madam." He replied coldly. His tone warned her to press him no further but she disregarded it.

"Then why is my good friend lying even now close to death in the Tower, Your Grace, her body all but wrenched apart by Wriothesly and others of the same breed? To what purpose Sire? What did they hope to gain?" She turned to Gardiner. "She has committed no sin my lord. What threat did she offer to you that you had to condone such vicious treatment?"

Gardiner's red face flickered uneasily for a moment as the King sat forward, obviously waiting for the man's reply. Henry knew of the torture. He condoned whatever methods were necessary in order to keep his subjects obedient, so long as the blame for those methods was not laid at his own feet, and no one sought to implicate the Queen. The Bishop trod warily. As always reminded that the King's innocence must not be tainted.

"The lady admitted reading literature of a treasonable nature Madam. Books of the New Learning were found in her possession and when questioned, she made no denial of her approval of the heretical works."

"And for this she must die?" Katherine cried incredulously. "For so small a sin? God's death my Lord, what wrong is there in it that every man should read and study as he please?"

"Such works question the King's position as Supreme Head of the Church, Madam." Gardiner replied soothingly. "If the King decrees that the Mass be read in Latin, that English translations of the Bible shall be banned as heretical, are we to believe Madam that you also are prepared to defy this wish? Are you in fact Madam setting yourself up as a better judge of what is right and good for the people of this realm than the King?"

Katherine ran her tongue over suddenly dry lips as she realised faintly how easily she had walked in the carefully laid trap. What more could Gardiner want than to trap her into an open confession of disobedience before the King? Blindly she swung away pressing her knuckles to her brow. Until now she had not realised just how insecure was that crown on her head. Knowing they waited she swallowed hard and knelt before the King.

"Your Grace, it is clear the Bishop has some personal motive for trying to make me say things which are not true and were never in my mind. I beg you as your most loving and humble wife to believe that I would never countenance any such treason against you. I have too great a love for you and respect most sincerely that wisdom and mercy which is equalled by no other." Her wide, dark eyes met his without flinching and Henry longed to take her into his arms, to have those fingers ease his aching brow.

"We believe no ill of you Kate."

Trembling with relief she took the hand he held out. "Then good Sire will you not spare for my sake, the life of that poor woman Mistress Askew?"

As if suddenly burned he released her again and fell back into his chair with a groan of pain.

"God's blood Madam can you not be content to keep your own neck safe? Must you always meddle? Try as I will I cannot forever protect you from your own folly."

"The Queen has much sympathy for the woman Sire. People will say if the prisoner is released that the King begins to be ruled by the Queen, that he indulges her whims."

Hatred and fury seethed through Katherine as Gardiner dealt this last sure blow against Anne Askew. Dizzily she swung to face him.

"I shall never understand my Lord how you can so fear to have the people educated. Or perhaps it is that you are so very much afraid that they will begin to understand what is preached to them by men such as yourself."

His eyes were expressionless as they poured scorn upon her.

"I obey the King, Madam, and do my best to see that his subjects likewise perform that same duty." He made a slight, half bow as if such respect would hide the true venom in his voice.

"Your Grace the lady is my friend, and never in her life did she intend disobedience . . ." Katherine turned again to Henry making a last appeal.

"Then she were better occupied in leaving such matters as book learning to men who are her betters Madam." Henry hissed coldly and then closed his lips firmly upon the matter.

Katherine knew it was over. She had failed to save Anne Askew. Wearily she swept a curtsey. "Have I your leave to retire Your Grace?"

Henry nodded, looking not at her but unseeingly over her head.

Anne was fated to die in the flames merely because she

had disagreed with men such as Gardiner, and because in the end she had proved stronger than their torture. She had refused to name the Queen as her confidante.

NINE

WINTER CAME to England with a vengeance in 1546. The Queen muffled herself warmly against the biting cold in fur-lined black velvet as she made her way to the Princesses' apartments.

Around her the court prepared for the Christmas merry-making. Men carried venison, beef and pigs to the kitchen. Pages with watering mouths followed with freshly killed chickens, ducks, pigeons and swan. From deep in the recesses of the Palace the smell of baking pies wafted up through dark stone stairways, and laughing maids carried boxes of imported peaches and oranges just come from Spain to the Great Hall.

Katherine moved silently along the passages, feeling the anticipation which seemed to build up around her as the festivities drew near, yet her own heart could take no pleasure in it, since Anne Askew had gone to the flames but a few weeks before.

The King did not withdraw his favour from the Queen as Gardiner had hoped, though it was clear that feelings were clearly strained between the royal pair. Not even the lowliest courtier could fail to note that the King was displeased, for he ignored the Queen at table except when it was necessary for him to speak and Katherine's eyes were often red from weeping as the battle between loyalty and conscience seemed to grow greater.

In the privacy of his apartments one evening, Henry took the Queen with kindliness onto his knee, crushing the rich brocade of her kingfisher gown as he fondled her gently and tried to persuade her to see reason. He knew what the Bishop was about, but how could even the King protect her if she still openly refused to forget these foolish notions of the New Religion.

"You can see Kate how plagued I am by the Church. It matters little to me and well you know it, what you read and speak of in the privacy of your own rooms. Not that I share your views mark you." He had added swiftly. "After all as head of the Catholic Church my duties are first to my people and where would England be if the King himself wavered from one faith to another?"

He looked into her serious eyes and playfully slapped her knee. "Can you not see the dangers if you persist sweetheart? I defend you by protesting your innocence in such matters to my Bishops, yet how can I expect them to be convinced when you raise that stubborn chin of yours Kate and openly challenge them with arguments which even I could find it hard to answer."

Her lips twitched. "Perhaps Your Grace is more than a little convinced by those arguments."

His face tightened and she realised her error.

"Nay Madam. Never think it." He tried to stand, spilling her from his knee and they confronted each other in awkward silence for a moment. "This New Learning is against all I ever held dear. Rome I can rid myself of, but don't let it lead you to think I can be persuaded to quit my faith with as much ease. From my wife I expect obedience, from the Queen I demand it and remind you only because

85

I love you Kate that I cannot forever stand between you and my Bishops."

"Those Bishops took from me a very dear friend Sire. A gentle woman who did not deserve to die. You cannot ask me to love a faith such as this?"

He swung away from her, grunting with pain and anger, realising that she remained stubborn as ever.

"God's blood Madam, how can I make you see . . ." He faced her, almost pleading for her understanding but she stood erect. "Would you have me divide England for your beliefs, which is what would happen if I showed myself to have any sympathy for them? Would you see us split as we were in the days before my father united the red rose and the white, except that the barrier this time be the Church?" Incredulously he watched her, saw the little furrow in her brow, the movement of her lips as she struggled to find some means of convincing him. But he gave her no time. He had no wish to be persuaded.

"Nay by God Madam, I'll not do it even for you. I take no side with you against my Bishops. It is enough for any man to battle with Rome, let alone with his own wife. Think on my warning and look to your own defence Kate. I can do no more."

Stunned by his anger she made some reply, not even hearing her own words. Then she had curtsied and been waved away. She withdrew still making excuses, still trying to regain his pleasure. But it was too late.

Tearfully she had promised to try to find some solution but as she made her way lost deep in thought along the passage, it still seemed that either one must obey blindly and without reason or one must question and seek for oneself the true way to God.

She entered the apartments and immediately the

Princesses Mary and Elizabeth rose with their ladies to make their curtseys. Katherine bid them rise and went forward to kiss the two young women on the cheek. Discreetly the ladies withdrew to sit with their embroidery on the wooden benches by the window.

Katherine seated herself, pushing back the heavy cloak and extending her hands to the blazing fire.

"I trust your headache is better this morning Mary?" She peered anxiously at the thin face before her and Mary flushed, as always wary of sympathy. In truth the migraine still plagued her but she nodded.

"I am well enough Madam."

Her fingers stabbed more energetically at the silk she was working upon.

Red haired Elizabeth laughed. "She fears to find herself confined to the sickroom for the festivities if she confesses the truth Your Grace." Regardless of the Princess's look of fury Elizabeth merely tugged at the folds of her green gown and adjusted the jewelled girdle which encircled her slender waist, falling to the hem of her gown weighed heavily by a gold pendant.

"Is this so Mary?" Katherine asked with quiet sympathy.

"I am become accustomed to the headaches Madam." The young woman shrugged off the questioning in her unusually gruff voice. "And I am not afeared to miss the proceedings since for me it is a time for prayer rather than over-indulgence anyway." The stiff Catholic pride of her Spanish mother reared its head in her words and Katherine smiled a little sadly.

"I will make up a posset of my own for you Mary, since I for one would be sorry to miss you at the celebrations. Now Elizabeth, let me see the presents you have there."

Obediently the young girl drew her stepmother to the

table. "This pomander is for Mary." She held up the golden orb to the light. "Of course it will be no surprise, but 'tis what she craves. See there are pearls and a ruby set on it. It will look well against her new burgundy gown."

"It will indeed." Katherine looked up to see a sudden smile on Mary's face and for a moment thought the woman seemed almost beautiful. She was glad the two Princesses had learned to live together in comparative harmony over the past few years. It was thanks to Queen Jane that they had found favour with the King and had been allowed to return to court during the brief year of her reign. Thought of Jane reminded her of Tom Seymour and for a moment her heart leapt uncomfortably in her breast. Quickly she bent to the table again.

"And what will you give the King, Mary?"

Somewhat reluctantly the Princess brought her work forward for the Queen's inspection. "This shirt Madam, embroided with my own hands, though I fear the work is not my best." Mary responded humbly.

Katherine picked up the garment feeling the soft white silk beneath her fingers. Closely she studied the delicate working of the Tudor rose in crimson and gold which decorated the front and collar of the shirt.

"But this is admirable Mary, and I know he will be greatly pleased. The King was ever pleased by skilful endeavour."

Elizabeth stood nibbling at her finger guiltily. "Alas I have only this velvet cushion. I am afraid it will serve only to remind him of the pain in his leg but then, I never seem able to please him anyway." Defiantly she waited for the Queen to remonstrate with her but Katherine did not.

"He will thank you a thousand times for it Elizabeth I am sure. Mayhap silently, but none the less he will do so.

There is not much these days that can ease the pain. This will at least bring him a little comfort."

"Perhaps my poor effort will go unnoticed in any event Madam, since the one person who could ever bring the King any real comfort is returned to court at last." Elizabeth laughed. "My Lord High Admiral brings a breath of life and youth with him. I think the festivities should be right merry this Christmas."

The Queen's white face stared at her blankly and the Princess wondered at the alarm she saw pictured there.

"Surely you knew that my Lord Seymour had returned Madam? 'Tis a week now since he came with the King's blessing, reluctantly given or otherwise for we all know the King could not forever withhold his favour from his brother-in-law."

"No, no, I did not know," Katherine answered faintly, despising herself for the bitter disappointment that he had not come to her.

Mary watched her silently and recognised the torment in the Queen's face. She too had longed for the strength of a man's arms and had been denied it because of her stubborn father.

"Should you not be rehearsing Edward in the song he is to sing on Christmas Day, Elizabeth?" Her voice rose shrilly.

"Lord save us, yes." Elizabeth rose abruptly from her stool. "The Prince is not over-patient when it comes to music, but the King has a keen ear and will take note of any error. Pray forgive me, Your Grace, if I take your leave. Young Edward must needs practise before he stands before the King."

"Tell me first, is his cough any better, Elizabeth?"

Katherine halted her step-daughter's progress with a gentle hand.

The Princess's red curls shook. "Nay, I think not, Madam. He is still much weakened after the measles which kept him to his bed for several weeks." She responded with obvious concern.

"Yes, I know. But thank God it was not the smallpox as the doctors first thought."

Mary crossed herself quickly as Katherine spoke.

"The King was much put about that he could not visit your brother, though it was to be expected. After all, His Grace's advisers will not allow your father to endanger his own life by entering the sick room."

"It is always so, Madam. We expect no other, for the King's health is of more import than any other." Elizabeth smiled as if to reassure the Queen, who realised even now that she still had much to learn of these children who were already hardened to the strict etiquette of the court.

"Edward must find it extremely dull, confined as he is to his apartments."

"Oh, I think he is not overly troubled, Madam. The physicians have allowed him to have visitors since the spots cleared, though the King may not yet attend him, of course, until all risk is completely gone, but Edward is content with his writing. Why, I believe he takes almost as much pleasure in penning a letter in French or Latin as he does from viewing the King's Men at Arms."

Katherine laughed. "We must see to it that he is well garbed against the cold when he reviews the troop, otherwise he will miss the Christmas revels. I shall ask His Grace for a sum from the privy purse so that you may purchase a warm cloak for your brother. What say you to that, Highness?"

Elizabeth clapped her hands with pleasure. "'Tis one expense the King will not begrudge, I am assured, Madam."

Mary glanced up from her work, her fingers hovering in mid-air. "Indeed the King would seem to begrudge our new mother no item at all, I think. It is become common gossip, Madam, that you interceded with the King on behalf of the University of Cambridge, which took courage indeed." Her lips smiled generously.

"It was but a small matter, Mary." Katherine pushed it aside, flushing. But her step-daughter would not be denied.

"Nay, I think it was not so small a matter, Madam," she insisted. "For if the King had taken the revenues of that University as he had intended when the realm was in such poor straits, those poor scholars would have been hard put to it to survive."

"I did no more than persuade your father that it were far better to advance learning, rather than crush it out of existence."

"He would not have been so readily persuaded by another's arguments, I think, Madam." Elizabeth laughed openly. "You cannot doubt that he will be doubly generous in so small a matter as a new cloak for his son?" Her mouth quivered mischievously and Katherine smacked her playfully.

"I may yet possibly contrive to win new gowns for my two daughters if I set my mind to it," she said with mock severity. "So save your pertness, my lady, lest I change my mind. And now I think you must attend your brother. He will welcome your company."

"Doubtless little Jane Grey our cousin has occupied his thoughts, Madam; they are like two studious mice together. I sometimes wonder how such young heads can contain so much knowledge."

Their faces became momentarily serious again, until Mary reminded her sister of her former intent.

"When our brother's music is as brilliant as his wit, then may you relax, sister. Until then I urge you to tutor him in earnest."

Elizabeth leapt to her feet again and swept towards the door, making a curtsy before she left.

Left alone with Mary, the Queen turned to wait patiently for her step-daughter to speak.

"Well, Mary, we are alone at last. Clearly something is troubling you. Shall we discuss it now?"

"I don't understand, Madam." The thin cheeks flamed with colour.

"No matter, Mary. You may speak plainly with me."

There were moments of uneasy silence as the Princess hesitated, faltered and finally took courage.

"Yes, it is true, Madam, there is something I must say. 'Tis the High Admiral . . . my Lord Seymour."

Katherine's heart seemed to pound, contracting violently. "What of him?"

Again the same pause as Mary picked nervously at the puffing of her false sleeve. "He was . . . you were . . ." The grey eyes flickered upwards in great agitation. "Madam, I cannot find the words to say it."

Katherine turned away, hoping thus to make it easier for her step-daughter to overcome her discomfort. "You have no reason to fear me, Mary. Say what you will. My anger was never unjustly raised, I think."

"I know it, Madam, but it makes the telling no easier." Her fingers strayed unthinkingly to the gold cross which hung at her neck. "My Lord Seymour once entertained hopes of making you his wife."

Katherine whitened visibly and spun to face her. "You cannot possibly have such knowledge."

"Forgive me, Madam. It is a secret well kept, but rumour is ever rife at court. Where others are blind I see much. 'Tis a habit cultivated during years when I found it necessary to defend myself against courtly malice. The King my father has a great love for his brother-in-law. It would take much to make him send my Lord away and I know Thomas Seymour went away unwillingly when you became Queen."

The Queen moved slowly away, considering the woman carefully. As always, she thought of Mary as a child, and indeed the Princess stood obediently with her head lowered, almost as if waiting for a scolding.

"You are shrewd, Mary. I always knew it. But having warned me of this knowledge, you must explain to me how you intend to use it."

Mary's eyes widened with horror. "Dear God, Madam, you misjudge me if you think I would use you ill. If the King is content to ignore it, who am I to cause mischief between you?"

"Then to what purpose . . ." Katherine began, confused by the response.

"Forgive me, Madam, if I presume to advise, but your feelings are very plain to one who . . . who knows of such things. You still care for the High Admiral?"

"I think you go too far, Highness. You forget yourself."

Mary raised a hand defensively as if to shield herself from the sharp rebuke. Her face appeared strained beneath the dark hood. "Nay, Your Grace, forgive me if I speak too plainly. It is because I love you that I must give this warning."

"Think you I am a child, Mary, to need such warnings?"

"In some things, Madam, I think you are even more innocent than myself, for all I am a spinster."

Katherine raised her head rebelliously, wishing she could find some convincing denial for the woman who met her gaze without flinching, but after a moment she bit her lip and turned away.

"I have been a good and faithful wife to your father these past months."

"None can deny you that, Madam, but it is easy enough when temptation is removed. My father was wise to send Lord Seymour from the court when he wed you."

Katherine's eyes widened as realisation dawned. "I could never be sure if the King knew that there was talk of marriage between myself and the High Admiral. I suspected, but nothing more, and could scarcely ask."

"God's teeth, Madam, for what other reason do you think he was sent from court? You have much to learn of the King. Why, even the merest suspicion that my Lord entertained such hopes would set him to hankering after the prize himself. He always craved the unobtainable. Did you never ask yourself why the King should suddenly choose you, Madam?"

Dizzily Katherine's mind sped back to the terror and misery the King had brought with him to Snape Hall that day when he had ridden unannounced to her house. Blindly she reached for a chair and sat with a hand pressed to her pounding heart. Yes indeed, she had wondered a million times why she had been raised to be Queen of England.

"I have been a fool, Mary. Yet I think the King does love me."

The Princess knelt beside her. "And so he does, Madam, even though it may not have been his first intent. Despite the gossips and the malicious intriguers, you have worked some magic upon the King. But you make the error of relying too much upon it. Already the bond between you is being slowly severed by troublemakers and God knows you give them ammunition enough to work with. All I ask is that you tread warily, and don't give them yet further opportunity to strike at you."

Katherine understood her meaning. "I have not seen Thomas Seymour for many months."

Mary laughed, but without humour. "My Lord Seymour was ever a law unto himself, Madam. He delights in such situations as this and would find it merry sport to woo you again, even beneath the King's very nose."

Horrified, Katherine pulled her hands away from Mary's, but the Princess was not to be silenced.

"I think perhaps you do not know my Lord Seymour as well as you think."

Swiftly the Queen rose and Mary fell back. "And I think, my Lady, that maybe jealousy directs your tongue rather than concern for my conscience."

Immediately it was said she regretted the words as Mary's face whitened. Too often had the Princess dreamed of marriage, only to have the hope snatched away by her ruthless father. And now it was too late. Silently she rose from the floor, watching as Katherine pressed a hand to her lips to keep back the sobs of misery.

"Don't reproach yourself, Madam. Those words are perhaps very close to the truth. Thomas Seymour was once the very height of my ambition. As a child I liked to imagine myself wed to a Prince and one day becoming a Queen in my own right, but as time went by and fate dealt less fairly with me, I began to realise that no country would look to me, labelled bastard by my own father, for its Sovereign. It was then that I allowed myself to think of

95

the Admiral as possible suitor. After all, a Princess may surely look so high." Her voice broke off and Katherine went forward but was shrugged aside. "I do not need your pity, Madam. Let me finish since it will perhaps warn you if nothing more. Thomas Seymour is an ambitious man. Aye, so ambitious that once he even ventured to think of taking me for his wife. And let me be the first to say it, I am no great catch save in the one respect that I still have my title." Her thin face twisted briefly in pain. "And I would have loved him right well."

"Mary, Mary," Katherine whispered softly, but she appeared not to hear.

"The world knows Edward is not strong. His cough grows worse. If aught should happen . . . You see, Madam, my Lord Seymour is prepared to marry where the greatest prize is." Bitterly she smiled. "I was foolish enough to believe he cared until I learned that he was also wooing my own sister. What better than to have two Princesses dangling, and the Lord knows Elizabeth received his advances well enough." She fell silent and stood looking down at the floor. "Perhaps I should be grateful that my father gave no serious thought to the match, for much as he loves Thomas Seymour he would not give his consent to such a marriage for a Princess of the Blood Royal."

Katherine's brain raced with shock and sick disbelief. Yet she couldn't doubt the obvious sincerity of Mary's words. Was it possible that she had not seen this side of Thomas Seymour? Her heart was torn between the undoubted truth of her step-daughter's words and the memory of those wonderful moments in his arms. Instinct cried out that she could not have been so deceived. She straightened up. At least now she was warned to be on her guard against those charms. Her position was precarious enough. At least this new knowledge might protect her from further errors. She moved towards the door and turned.

"I thank you, Mary. I know what it has cost you to say these things. If it is any consolation, you may be sure that I shall remember them."

The Princess made a deep curtsey and remained thus until the Queen had gone.

Katherine moved automatically towards her own rooms. Her mind whirled.

And yet he would have gained nothing by marrying me. It was said over and over again. My Lord Seymour will marry where the greatest prize is. Mary's voice seemed to echo. Furiously she clasped her hands to her ears and began to run, suddenly eager to reach the quiet privacy of her own rooms. It was true—she had much to learn, even now, about the ways of men.

TEN

"TOM." THE KING leaned suddenly forward, his plump face creasing into an expression of childlike joy as his watery eyes beheld the figure who strode into the hall. "Tom, lad, so you've come back to me at last." Eagerly his hands reached forward as if to bring the man quickly closer to him. For once he could even ignore the pain in his leg.

With a laugh the High Admiral ran forward, and when he would have made a formal bow the King reached out and grasped him in those still amazingly powerful hands, pulling him forward.

"Nay, Tom lad, don't kneel to me. Hal is too pleased to see you waste time with such formalities." In a bearlike embrace the two clung together. Henry's eyes ran with tears of unadulterated joy as he clasped the very breath of life to him again. He sniffed and held Tom Seymour from him, scanning the handsome face. "By the Lord, Tom, it's been a long time. Too long. Why did you stay from our sight for so many months?"

The Admiral felt himself shaken by the hamlike fists and fought to hide the shock he felt as he saw the pain and age eaten into that face in so short a time.

"Nothing less than your own command would have driven me away, Sire," he reminded Henry and the King's small lips pursed suddenly as he recalled the reason for his sending Tom from him.

"Aye, well the King must use his best Ambassador to good advantage, lad, and you were needed elsewhere, much as I longed to have you close at hand." His cheeks flushed a little as he gave the lie. Warily for a second he searched the handsome face as if it might give him the answer to some question, but the blue eyes laughed boldly back at him.

"Then I can but hope Your Grace will not need to send me away again too soon. Foreign courts are dismal places when Kings have not the wit to share a friendly jest."

Henry glowed with pleasure. "So 'tis good to be back with your old Harry, is it, lad?"

"Can you doubt it, your Grace? My heart is always in England with my King, no matter how many miles are between us."

Henry blew his nose violently, jarring the leg suddenly. A cry of pain escaped his lips and Tom watched as his white face fell back, seeing the teeth bite into colourless lips.

Deftly he placed a cushion on the small stool and lifted the King's leg gently on to it. The act reminded him instantly of Kate who must constantly perform that same service.

With an effort Henry dragged himself back to the present. "Thank you lad. Not many have so gentle a touch." Furtively he probed the wound as if willing it to cease its torture.

"And how does the Queen, Sire?" Their minds flew instinctively to that same person. Henry's glance flickered away momentarily and the Admiral noted it with sudden foreboding. He thought Chancellor Wriothesely seemed to draw suddenly closer but as he looked up the man's face showed no change in expression.

"Have you not seen Kate, Tom?" Henry queried as if surprised.

"My first duty is to yourself Your Grace ." Tom replied with practised ease. "Forgive me if I presume too much but I thought my bond with the King to be something special. Nothing shall ever come before it."

"And so it is special Tom." Now that his beloved brother-in-law stood before him again he could afford to laugh at those rumours which had begun to haunt him of late. He turned a scathing glance upon Wriothesely who shuffled uneasily.

The Chancellor fought down his panic. Clearly he would have to find some other means to work upon the King, for Henry would believe no ill of this handsome fellow who could match his every mood. If he could not use hints and rumour against the lady, then other means must be found. Silently he retreated into the shadows.

"You must present yourself to the Queen, Tom. She will wish to welcome you back to court. I know she once had a sisterly fondness for you.'

Thomas Seymour lowered his head, hiding a glimmer of amusement in his eyes. "If Your Grace commands it I will present myself to the Queen this very day."

"We do command it Tom. Kate will be pleased to see an old friend. It will cheer her up a little, her spirits are lowered just lately. She's not at all the lively little thing we used to know."

It was obviously a complaint against the Queen and he noted the sudden tightening of Henry's mouth with a feeling of panic.

"Is the Queen not well Your Grace?"

"Well?" Henry blinked. "Aye, she's well enough Tom. Would I could say it were otherwise, that she ailed because she carried my babe but it isn't so."

He wondered how a man could so deceive himself. Only one man believed the King capable of getting a woman with child, and that was the King himself.

"There is time enough to think of babes surely Sire? The Queen is still young and yourself full of vigour."

"True Tom, very true." Henry could still convince himself of that fact when he chose to. "Though I had thought by now ... ah well, no matter."

"Perhaps the Queen needs a change of air. Fresh surrounds and good country air can work miracles."

Henry drummed with his fingers on the arm of his chair and his eyes narrowed. " 'Tis not a change of air the Queen needs Tom. I wish it were so simple. What the lady needs is a change of heart and a stern lesson in wifely duty."

Until that moment Thomas Seymour had not realised how well the seeds of discontent had been sown in the King's heart. "The Queen was surely never lacking in that respect Sire." He dared to prompt.

"I wish it were so, but these past weeks the Queen has

100

again and again undermined our authority Tom. God's blood man, shall I be defied by a mere woman and have the people say I am ruled by my own wife?"

"I cannot believe Her Grace would knowingly offend ..."

"Her Grace has repeatedly chosen to defy the King's wishes in the matter of religion my Lord." Bishop Gardiner cut in swiftly, appearing suddenly from behind the King's shoulder, like some vulture in his black robes.

"Aye Tom, it was so." Henry nodded. "You know lad I care not for myself how the Queen spends her time ..."

Gardiner dared to break in upon his words. "But if the Queen encourages the New Learning my Lord, Thus putting in doubt His Grace's right as Supreme Head of the Church, how long will it be before the people begin to heed such treason which undoubtedly it would be termed in any other."

Casually Thomas Seymour drew off the fine hand-stitched gloves, playing for time as his mind sought for some way to extricate her from this obvious trap. He flicked the gloves against his thigh-length riding boots, dispersing clouds of dust gathered on London's muddy tracks and sat with apparent unconcern on a chair beside the King, almost as if he hoped that such a position might remind the other of his entitlement to that place.

"Treason is a strong word Bishop. Are you not over-dramatising this affair?"

"Perhaps you can find a better one my Lord?" Wriothesely suggested sarcastically.

"May I ask then if you have proof of such acts gentlemen?" His eyes appraised the Bishop coolly, and Gardiner flushed.

"We shall find it Sir."

Henry slammed a fist down heavily on to the table at his side, rocking it dangerously. "God's teeth you forget yourselves gentlemen. It is for the King to decide what be treason or otherwise. We do not need to be advised by you or any others on such matters. There was never any woman less sinful than the Queen, my Lords. Indeed you would do well to take a lesson from my Katherine in humility. Do you think we would heed such gossip against her, God's death will I look for proof of treason against so gentle a wife?" He blustered out the words as he realised how close Kate was suddenly come to tragedy. Despising them all, he remembered her sweet face and couldn't bear to have yet another Queen torn from him by men such as these. Only at the back of his mind did the thought linger that in the eyes of the world he was already the 'butcher King of England'. How would Europe look upon the death of yet another wife?

"Your Grace is over-indulgent as always." Gardiner reproved him with amazing courage. "But it was ever a failing of our Sovereign."

As always Henry was blinded by such flattery. "True, Bishop. But in the matter of the Queen we shall say no more. Her Grace is a good and devoted wife in all respects. I am well content with the match."

"As you wish Sire, though my fears are not entirely without reason. I speak only for your protection."

"I think we can safely judge what is harmful to our person Bishop." Henry's chin lifted with sudden severity but as usual Gardiner was determined on his say and disregarded the warning signs.

"Her Grace has a great influence upon the royal children. An increasing influence since she took upon herself the responsibility of their education. How will it appear I wonder should the young Heir and his sisters choose to follow the dictates of the Queen rather than the King their father in so grave a matter as religion?"

Henry opened his mouth to speak and then obviously thought better of it. He leaned back in his chair and watched the Bishop through narrowed eyes. There was truth in it. Kate did instruct the Prince and Princesses in such matters. "We had not thought of it Gardiner, but you are right of course. The Queen has our consent to tutor them as she thinks fit."

"The Queen cares for the royal children as if they were her own Your Grace. Surely none can find fault with that?" Thomas Seymour reminded him pointedly.

"Far better were she occupied in having babes of her own my Lord, rather than converting the King's off-spring to her heretical beliefs." Wriothesely could not hide a small smirk of triumph as he saw the point find its target. "But perhaps my Lord Seymour feels a certain sympathy for the Lady in this matter?"

Henry watched the reaction carefully. He saw the faint colour steal up in Thomas Seymour's neck above the scarlet cloak.

"The Lord Chancellor seems anxious to find treason where none is intended Your Grace. Am I to believe myself also accused simply because I defend the Queen, yet have scarce set foot in England after an absence of several months?" He rose heatedly to stand before Henry waiting for some reassurance.

"The Chancellor defends his King, Tom. It is for you to decide where your loyalties lie."

"My loyalty was never before in doubt Your Grace. If I defend the Queen now, 'tis because as the King's wife Madam is surely entitled to that respect."

103

"The Queen's Grace forfeits the right to that respect by her continued wilful disregard of her husband's wishes my Lord. The King has been more than patient." Gardiner addressed his words to Henry.

"So I have Tom. So I have. Kate is a good woman, but even the Queen shall not meddle in such profound matters as the faith of my people. My son shall one day be King. He must learn to look to men for advice, rather than to women who know little enough of anything."

"But the fact that the Queen instructs the children in religious matters is scarcely proof of treason Sire?"

"It is treason enough when Madam obliges the young Prince and Princesses to translate forbidden works into English my Lord."

Thomas Seymour whirled to face him. "And have you seen these works my Lord?"

Gardiner crimsoned. "I know of them Sir."

"Ah, but you cannot produce them here, so that the King may judge for himself whether they be treasonable or simply harmless schooling? His Grace is surely capable of deciding for himself whether the Queen exceeds her duties." He drew closer to Henry. "May I ask Sire, have you seen for yourself such evidence?"

The pale eyes veered towards Gardiner. "Nay Tom. We have not. Well Bishop, am I to accept mere words yet again as proof of treason? It is a grave charge whomsoever it be levelled against."

The Bishop of Winchester shot a look of venom at the High Admiral.

"You shall have the proof Your Grace, and more. The Queen is known to possess books which are forbidden."

"Then produce them Sir, if you can." Seymour retaliated.

Henry relaxed as the battle of wits reached stalemate. It seemed these days that he was constantly being pushed hither and thither by controversy concerning the Queen. There were times, when his leg pained him, when he knew that only Kate's gentle fingers could ease the torment. At such times it filled him with terror to think he might be deprived of his sweet nurse. And at other times, when he was mercifully free from pain he could almost wish himself free again. After all, Kate had so far failed in that most important of duties, she had failed to give him an heir. There were plenty more pretty faces about the court. A mistress? The thought crossed his mind and was quickly banished. No, dear God. It had to be a wife. A seventh wife, for his sons must be legitimate. Quickly he jerked himself back to the present, shocked to know how easily he had already dismissed Kate. Ah but if he were only twenty years younger so that he might sweep her off her dignified little feet and carry her to that huge bed, as he had done with Anne . . . and Kathryn . . . His thoughts wandered aimlessly. He looked up suddenly at his brother-in-law. Handsome, young. Kate's age, full of life. Jealousy welled up in him and he waved them all angrily away, dribbling spittle onto his beard.

"Go away and quarrel elsewhere gentlemen. Yes you too brother. I am heartily wearied of these arguments. Let me have some peace for so far no one has shown me any proof of treason in the Queen. Kate is a good woman, I wish to God the rest of you were as innocent as she."

The Chancellor's mouth snapped shut on further comment. Wriothesely, Gardiner and Thomas Seymour bowed and left the apartments. Beyond the door they paused, each unsatisfied.

"Well my Lord Chancellor, Bishop. You have contrived a

deal of mischief in my absence from court. The King and his wife were happy enough just a few months ago, and already your mischief is coming between them. Is the King never to have any peace?"

"If there is mischief my Lord High Admiral, then 'tis of the Queen's making. She has but to conform as any wife to her husband's wishes."

"Yes and even I can see that it would suit you well to have a Catholic on the throne Bishop, one who will work to your own advantage."

"I think my Lord you mistake our motives. We wish only to save the King from further tragedy. After all he has been mistaken before in his choice of wife."

"And you will show him yet another such mistake eh my lords? And the Queen's only error is that her faith challenges yours?" He laughed. "I think I understand well enough gentlemen. I bid you good day. The air in here is suddenly become offensive." With a slight bow he hurried away.

"It is Sir Thomas Seymour, Madam." Lady Herbert volunteered the information to her sister as she spoke over her shoulder from the door of the apartment.

Katherine rose from her chair in such haste that the book she was reading fell from her lap and clattered to the floor where it lay unheeded. Margaret bent quickly to retrieve it, clasping the slim volume beneath the brilliant blue of her sleeve.

"I'll not see him. Bid him go away." White faced she stood listening as the message was conveyed. Anne Herbert seemed to be arguing for the veil of her green hood moved vigorously.

"The High Admiral says it is most urgent." She turned with obvious regret to the Queen.

"I am sure it is." Katherine broke in, her voice shrill with hysteria. "But I cannot see Lord Seymour at present."

The door was pushed suddenly open and it fell with a resounding bang against the wall. With a violent shiver the Queen saw his tall figure advance into the room and stride to confront her. Her ladies retreated slowly as if driven by some hidden force.

His dark head bowed formally and then was raised immediately to pierce her own desolate face which trembled with the closeness of threatening tears.

"Lord Seymour . . ." It was scarcely more than a whisper as she saw the anger in his face.

It stung him still to receive such formality at those gentle hands which had once welcomed his embrace. He saw the fear in her dark eyes and understood it, but worse, much worse he detected a hint of doubt, of mistrust.

"I am here with the King's consent Madam." He seemed anxious to reassure her.

"I am sure of it my Lord, though I think it was not necessary to . . ." Her voice broke off. It sounded strained even to her own ears. His lips tightened and he glanced about the room, becoming suddenly aware of the women who hovered uncertainly, watching. With a frown of annoyance he faced the Queen again.

"I would speak with you alone Kate. What I have to say is not for all ears."

Her heart quickened again at the familiar use of her name upon his lips but she hid the emotion well.

"I warned you many months ago my Lord that I could never again receive you under such circumstances." For a second she seemed to hesitate, hoping for his understanding but he didn't respond to the gesture. "My position was precarious enough then, 'tis doubly so now. Will you endanger me further for the mere . . ." She faltered. "The mere sport of winning the unobtainable?" Her low voice trailed away, cut off by the tightening of her throat and more by the look of disbelief in his eyes.

Sharp fingers cut into her wrist and she winced with pain. "Do you truly believe that?" He questioned bitterly. "Can you really have learned in so short a time to think it of me?" She lowered her eyes afraid of his anger. He was closer now and she looked beyond him to Lady Herbert who stood helplessly by, not understanding and unable to help. "Who made you believe it?" He almost shook her in his rage. Waiting for her to deny it.

Shame surged through her as she remembered Mary's words, and yet however truthfully Mary had spoken, in her own heart she knew now that there could be no more doubts. Thomas Seymour did love her. There could be no reward for him in loving Katherine Parr and much less in loving the King's wife. Such folly could only bring death. Quickly she reached out to grasp his sleeve, horrified by the pain she had inflicted.

"Forgive me Tom. My nerves are gone to pieces. Between the King and Gardiner I am one way or another sure to lose my mind, or indeed my head."

He followed her to the window. "Then at least you recognise your enemies. I came to warn you, Gardiner will somehow find evidence to prove that you try to influence the royal children towards the New Faith. I was with the King when he mentioned works which they translate at your request."

She laughed incredulously. "But dear God who can find treason in that?"

"Need you ask?" His smooth brow furrowed. "Don't credit the Bishop with any feelings of conscience Kate. He will send you to the block without hesitation if it will further his own ends."

Her hands moved in a violent spasm to her white throat. Her shoulders trembled suddenly. "Has the King so little love for me that he will listen to such tales?"

Thomas Seymour beat his fist against the oak panelling. "Kate he is an old man. A weary man. A King who tries to keep a last hold upon youth by believing himself still capable of getting a son, and who must always believe himself still master in England. He is blind to Gardiner's persuasion, doesn't see himself being led to decisions. And even if he did, he would not admit himself too weary to prevent it."

Katherine turned away, trying to force out some words. "And I thought I was safe so long as the King loved me. I counted on it, yet now you show me that I must fight these men, even my husband alone if I am to save my neck?" She turned to face him with the question, her eyes brimming with tears. Her body felt numb with terror.

"At least you are warned of one means they will try to use against you."

"The King's children you mean?" Wearily she turned from him. "Yes I can perhaps defend myself against that charge, having been forewarned. But Gardiner will not let it rest there now that he is openly determined to be rid of me. They will use any means at their disposal and God knows this is why I must say again Tom, don't seek me out. For both our sakes." Desperately she tried to make him understand. "If they can contrive the Queen's death Tom, they will certainly not hesitate at yours."

He moved quickly, pulling her behind the velvet hangings which divided the large room from a smaller ante-chamber. Momentarily they were alone and she struggled in sudden panic to release herself from his grasp.

"Tom are you mad? Even my own women I cannot be sure of." Her hands tried to force him away but he held her tightly.

"Don't deny me a worthy farewell Kate." He forced her chin up so that she had to met his gaze. "I saw the doubt in those eyes and at least if I must go I have the right to know who put such a question there."

She twisted away but he jerked her back to him again. Guilt flickered for a second in her eyes and he saw it.

"Mary." She whispered it and he stared at her disbelieving.

"Mary? In heaven's name why? What tales can she tell which would make you doubt?"

Katherine hesitated. "Is it true . . . Is it true that you once hoped to wed the Princess and that you even ventured to woo the Lady Elizabeth with that same purpose in mind?"

She could never be sure whether his answering laugh came just a shade too quickly for sincerity.

"Kate can you honestly believe it? It is true the King dwelt on the idea of a marriage between myself and Mary. Call it guilty conscience if you will, after all he denied her the marriage bed so many times and for so long that perhaps he thought to compromise somehow by offering me as husband." He shrugged. "A poor choice you might think for the daughter of a King of England but what other was there? I wooed the lady, half-heartedly I'll admit. But can you seriously imagine Mary as my wife, Kate? God's oath, she is a virgin born and a virgin like to die."

The Queen coloured. "But as you say, the lady was not

110

to blame for that. And what of Elizabeth? Was she too just a game?"

He turned from her with a careless lift of the shoulders. "Aye if you will. But that young woman has her father's spirit. She is wild and impetuous and forgive me if I say it but the Lady Elizabeth is a flirt. We were never lovers, God knows even I would not have dared with a Princess of England, we were not even sweethearts except perhaps in the Lady's heart. Believe me Kate, it was never more than a childish game with either of them."

Katherine's lips puckered in a brief smile of relief. "I am glad Tom. I could not have borne it if . . ." The words were cut off abruptly as his mouth crushed down on hers. For a few brief seconds she clung to him and then broke away, gasping for breath. Her face was flushed. "Please Tom, no. Remember my women." Her hand was pressed to her lips as if to remove all trace of the kiss. "Please go now, before too much harm is done."

He released her gently. "I have no choice have I Kate?"

She shook her head.

"But I shall watch and wait, and if the time ever comes . . ."

Quickly her hand was pressed to his lips. "Don't say it Tom. Even to think of the King's death is treason in these times. I know you will be close at hand. It is enough. Remain in favour with the King my love, in this way you can help me best."

"I wish there were some better way, some positive thing I could do . . ."

"No my love. If you openly supported me it would only bring both of us to the block. Better this way."

"As you will Kate." His lips brushed against her fingers. Quickly she withdrew her hand and stepped back beyond the velvet hangings and into the room where her ladies sat.

"Goodbye, My Lord Seymour. It is good to see you at court again. The King I know will be much comforted by your presence."

His head bent formally over her extended hand, then he was gone. Katherine watched, staring blankly at the door. Her thoughts were torn between fear for her own insecurity and a longing to have his arms comfort her. She sighed and turned away just in time to catch the watchful glance of one of her woman.

Lady Russell's lashes flickered swiftly downwards to her embroidery again. It was little enough incident in itself, yet Katherine felt suddenly burdened by yet more problems to which there seemed no possible solution.

ELEVEN

THE KING stood at the window of his apartment, looking down onto the lawns below. With a faraway expression in his watery eyes he watched the young girl with the tossing dark head and the rose-coloured gown which whirled about her ankles as she ran from the embraces of an eager young man. For a brief moment she turned, laughed and glanced upwards and Henry's heart seemed to freeze in his breast.

"Anne." He murmured soundlessly and felt the hot tears well up in his eyes. Almost did he leap forward to call her name, until feeling suddenly foolish he fell back again, hammering his fist miserably against the wall. Of course it was not Anne. It was just that for one brief moment . . . He

112

looked again. The girl evaded the young man's grasp and with a musical laugh swept a deep curtsey in the King's direction before turning to run with the fleet-footed steps of a young deer across the grass.

The King's frown gave way to a sudden doubtful smile. Hands on hips he watched the maid's graceful flight. She couldn't be more than twenty, her body was slender, tall and supple. This much his experienced eye discerned at once. Many years ago Anne had made such a reckless, uncaring obeisance before him, as if to boast, to taunt and show how little she cared that he was King. This girl had that quality and she had boldly sent out the challenge.

His heart began to pound. Not for a long time had his blood quickened at the sight of a pretty face. With a snort of disgust he realised that he had of late begun to believe himself to be growing old. He, Henry of England old. Past bedding a saucy wench. His thickened frame eased painfully forward to lean from the window in order to catch a better sight of her. He must see better that face. Remember it and look for her again. Too old indeed! With a laugh of defiance he straightened up. The Tudor was not yet incapable of taking a mistress to his bed when the desire arose in him. He would show them all, those who thought him an old man to be pampered, pitied and cosseted. His small lips tightened. By the Lord with such a creature he could still beget a dozen heirs.

The crimson silk of his shirt rustled slightly, the diamond buttons catching the light as he turned suddenly. Sunlight streamed through the window, giving the now paler but still golden hair a vaguely ethereal look.

In silence he contemplated his wife.

Katherine's dark blue gown billowed stiffly about her as she sat with her head bent over her work. The dark hair

113

flowed long and free over her shoulders restricted only by the French hood. Her face was white, colourless. Her usually bright eyes dull and the full lips drooped a little.

With a frown Henry realised that in some subtle way she had begun to change. No longer did he see the youthful, eager woman, the frightened nymph of Snape Hall. Compared to that other laughing creature she seemed suddenly a cruel reminder of encroaching age.

"What, sulking Kate?"

The words jolted suddenly on her ears and she started, pricking her finger viciously with the needle. With a cry she dropped the work as spots of brilliant blood welled up from the tiny wound. Her eyes widened in her pale face as she stared upwards, trying to fathom that keen scrutiny.

"Your Grace?" She questioned with sudden fear.

"You sulk Kate." He repeated churlishly. "We are accustomed to more attentiveness from our wife, some chatter however trivial. Perhaps you are bored by our presence Madam?" Boorishly he seemed to want to find fault, to chide her for his own feelings of sudden restriction. He had to blame someone . . .

Katherine rose swiftly from her chair putting aside the work. She stood feeling suddenly guilty as those pig-like eyes seemed to accuse her, and yet of what she could not be sure.

"It was not my intent to offend you Henry." She replied honestly. "If I am silent it is because I do not wish to intrude. You were clearly deep in thought."

Grey pools of ice surveyed her thoughtfully. "Left to our own devices we needs must occupy ourselves somehow Madam."

She bit her lip at the unfairness of his words but dared

offer no reproach. This formality, this sudden deliberate attempt to provoke an argument sickened her.

"Perhaps Your Grace would like me to sing . . . to play the lute?" Quickly she sought to divert him but Henry snappishly waved her to silence.

"I have musicians Madam more competent than yourself."

That stung her. It had always been a joke between them that her voice had no great merit when his own was so excellent, but never before had he found fault with her because of it.

He hobbled painfully to a bench and was about to sit and ease the pain of his throbbing leg when he thought better of it and angrily moved away.

Full of concern she went towards him. 'Shall I put a fresh dressing on the leg for you. Doctor Wendy gave me a new cream which is said to work miracles."

"Nay Madam, the leg is well enough." Feverishly he pushed her away, hating himself momentarly for the pain he saw in her eyes. He sweated profusely in the immense padding of his doublet and short coat and tugged at the collar of his shirt. Poor Kate. She couldn't understand that he must once again prove himself a man, the lusty Harry of England. He was not old.

Young laughter rose to his ears from the garden below and it drove him still further to hurt her.

"Must you always fuss and pamper us Madam? We are not yet ready for our tomb, or is it that you would hasten us to it?" Through narrowed slits he saw the tears glisten on her lashes. Red faced he looked away. "Are your hands so idle? Does the Queen have no other duties in my court?"

Swallowing back the lump in her throat she nodded, clasping her hands before her in an attempt to appear calm.

"Since Your Grace has seen fit to deprive me of your children's company . . ."

The obvious rebuke stung him. "It would seem we acted wisely Madam. It was not our intent that you should seek to influence our children to your own heretical beliefs."

A gasp of horror broke from her. "I did no more than to have the Princess translate a passage of the Bible Your Grace."

"Knowing full well Madam that we have forbidden the reading of the book."

Her voice rose in retaliation. "What is forbidden one year in this realm would seem to be the law in the next." Bluntly she snapped out the words and instantly regretted them as she saw his face purple with rage.

"Do you question me Madam? Do you think to teach your King in matters of faith what be right and wrong? Are you yourself so learned?"

Shaking in every limb she lowered her eyes. "I set myself up as no judge Sire, but in no manner can I see the harm in allowing your poorer subjects to read for themselves the English translation of the Bible. Indeed is it not possible they may thank you for giving that right?" Her voice trailed away as she saw the futility of her arguments.

"Methinks you would have the people question our very right as Head of the Church, Madam?"

Her heart missed a beat. Oh, foolish, foolish woman, she cried silently. To have walked so readily into the very trap you must avoid. She shook her head. "Nay, Your Grace, this is one matter of which I am very sure. My faults are many, since I am only a woman and of little intelligence, but never, never would I persuade the people to dispute that undoubted right." She knelt suddenly before him, taking him by surprise, and she remained with her head lowered. "Your Grace my husband is the true Head of the Church and never have I argued otherwise."

"Hm." He looked down at her uncertainly. That much at least was true, and still, though he would not have admitted it, he could still feel that tiny thrill which came to him as a lesser mortal knelt at his feet, looking to him for mercy. "Yet we do think you do take it upon yourself too often to correct us, Kate."

His familiar use of her name sent a flood of relief through her. Perhaps she may yet defend herself and win his approval.

"I am but a woman, Sire. A poor creature who thinks to learn a little wisdom by questioning a great man of unsurpassed knowledge. Where else would the Queen find so worthy a tutor than in her own husband?"

His heart swelled with self-conceit as he accepted without question the truth of her words. Swiftly he bent to raise her, puffing and gasping with pain and excess weight.

"My dear Kate, how can I be angered when your only sin is to foolishly hope to understand such complex matters? I misjudged you, sweetheart. 'Tis commendable in you to think of acquiring such knowledge, yet I think it were wiser to leave such things to your betters." He patted her hand tolerantly.

"Indeed I see that, Your Grace, and I beg your forgiveness."

" 'Tis given, Kate, 'tis given." Clumsily he kissed her forehead. "But be warned, sweetheart, never think to come again between the King and his conscience."

"And his Bishops," she murmured beneath her breath.

Henry frowned but did not catch the words, and as she made her curtsey he gave it no further thought.

"Aye, leave us, Kate. Take your stitching elsewhere and

occupy yourself in more womanly pleasures in future."

"I will, indeed, my Lord." Grateful for the dismissal, she scooped up her work and fled the room.

In the doorway she collided with Bishop Gardiner, who stood aside with a curt bow as she sped past. Her gaze flickered over him contemptuously, then she was gone, leaving him feeling as always that she pitied him.

"Ah, Gardiner." Henry beckoned him in and returned to his place by the window.

Gardiner went to his side and looked down, following the King's gaze. His eyes also lingered upon the lovely creature who flaunted her charms so obviously before his master.

"You have business with me, my Lord?" Henry questioned him half-heartedly. It was plain his thoughts were far away.

Gardiner studied him in silence, watching the flabby face wrinkle with pleasure as the girl waved. Henry's hand rose in reply and then, in an impulsive gesture, he pulled a ring from his finger and tossed it down to her. Delight shone in her face as she caught the costly jewel, pressed it briefly to her lips and then, laughing up at him, slipped it onto her finger. Henry's lips bubbled with laughter. He seemed totally unaware of the Bishop.

" 'Tis nothing of importance, Your Grace," Gardiner belatedly answered the King. "Merely to inform Your Grace that the town is being searched as you directed for forbidden literature."

"Aye, well, report to me when it is done . . ." Henry murmured, caring not one jot for the Bishop and his search. He reached out suddenly, putting an arm about the man's shoulders. "A beautiful day, is it not, Bishop? A day when the sun shines and the birds sing. It makes a man feel full of life. Can you not feel it, Gardiner, a certain something in the air?"

Indeed there was a certain something, Gardiner thought. Though whether it be the brightness of the day or the virginal youthfulness of that maid, he could not be sure. Over the King's shoulder he strained to catch a glimpse of her. Saw the gown billow like a newly opened rose and her dark hair flung about by a breeze. Aye, there was something in the air all right.

"I am pleased to see Your Grace restored to good health at last. Though 'tis only what we expected with the warmer weather, Sire." He murmured the expected response.

"I could almost take it into my head to hunt again, Bishop, and by the Lord, that's something I haven't done these many months." Henry seemed thrilled with the idea and Gardiner hid his concern. "But perhaps we will think on it first." Grudgingly the King realised that he sped on too fast. "When the ulcer is fully closed, then we shall gather us a fair escort and take to horse again." Once more he was far away, picturing that slender body in riding habit galloping at his side.

Gardiner silently bowed and retreated. His shrewd eyes watched until the last moment the King's suddenly youthful face. Here indeed was a further incident he might put to use against the proud Katherine Parr. Let her not think herself too secure. The King had taken a sixth wife, but it was not inconceivable that there might be a seventh Queen of England.

TWELVE

LADY HERBERT'S gown of kingfisher brocade, stitched with pearls and sapphires, trailed heavily over the floor as she advanced almost furtively along the Great Hall towards her sister. Her pretty face was troubled, though she did her best to hide it by smiling at the courtiers assembled there in small groups. Her wide turned-back sleeves hung like huge butterfly wings against the folds of her gown, showing to full advantage the silver and crimson tighter false sleeve beneath, ending in a froth of finest Brussels lace at her wrist. Her slender form bent in a formal homage as she came to the Queen's side.

"Madam, I must speak with you most urgently." Rising, she touched the Queen's arm and Katherine turned.

Her shrewd eyes saw immediately the agitation in Anne Herbert's face, and slowly, as if unconcerned, she moved away from her ladies, bidding her sister follow.

"Something is amiss, Anne. I can see it." Her lips smiled so that none should suspect they discussed anything of importance. Gently she led the way towards the window seat, where she sat and urged Lady Herbert to do the same. "We cannot be heard here, but be careful. Smile. Sharp eyes watch." Katherine laughed and smoothed the folds of black velvet around her slim waist. "I have my suspicions that Gardiner has his spies even among my own women. Ah, there, see for yourself if I am correct. Lady Russell draws away from her companions and moves in this direction." As if unconcerned, she leaned forward to inspect the jewelled medallion which hung at her sister's waist. Over her head Anne Herbert also noted the imperceptible movements of that Lady.

"Yes, you are right, though if the Lady hopes to remain unnoticed she must fail sadly in that puce satin. 'Tis our fortune, perhaps, that Gardiner sets no abler spy to watch, though whether she is a spy or 'tis just her busybodying way we cannot be sure. Still, better beware."

"I am continually on my guard these days, Anne. But tell me quickly what troubles you. I dare not linger here too long or someone will begin to suspect. I did promise to speak with Lady Petre, who would have me stand as godmother to her infant. She hovers impatiently already, I see."

"Bestow the child with your own name and I'll wager the mother will be amply pleased. I only wish our own problems were so easily solved."

From deep in the folds of her gown Lady Herbert withdrew a small volume. She allowed it to rest, still half concealed, upon the bench between herself and the Queen.

With a slight gasp of alarm Katherine's eyes flickered downwards and then quickly away again. "In God's name, Anne, have you taken leave of your senses?" Her attention seemed to be rivetted upon her women, though she saw nothing. "Will you condemn me with your own actions before the King?"

Anne Herbert covered the book with her gown and bit her lip nervously.

"Forgive me. If there were any other way I would not have come to you, but the town is being ransacked. Gardiner and Wriothesely have ordered the searching of every house for literature such as this and, by our Lord, it come too close to our own doorstep. I could not turn my friends away when they came to me for help."

"But what can you or any of us do against the Bishop?"

Anne shrugged despondently. "Little enough, I know, but this book is precious, which is why it was brought to me. Perhaps in the vain hope that I might be able to keep it safe. I see now it was a terrible mistake, but my friends would not see the book burned, and to keep it where it will be found means certain death."

The Queen turned away from the chattering groups of women and looked again at the book. Her fingers ran over the much thumbed pages.

"Tyndale's translation of the New Testament, and much loved, obviously, by its owner," she murmured, her face betraying the joy she felt.

"Dearly loved indeed, Madam," her sister affirmed. "My friend is no coward, but will it serve the New Faith to have its followers burned as heretics? Better, surely, to hide such books and fight on, for the day will surely come when every man is free to choose for himself what he shall read."

"No one prays for that more than I, Anne. But what can I do?"

"If you will conceal the book until the search is over ..." Lady Herbert began eagerly.

"But you know how much I am already plagued by Gardiner, Anne."

"I know it well enough, Katherine, but as Queen you are at least exempt from his prying."

"Yes, but for how long?"

The two women sat in silence, each depressed by the seemingly inescapable movement of events, until reluctantly Lady Herbert began to conceal the book again within her gown. Slowly she rose.

"I should not have come to you with this. God knows you have more to fear than the rest."

Katherine jerked herself swiftly back to the present, realising that her sister was about to take her leave. "No, wait. You did right. After all, the people look to me for support in this. If I deny them, where else will they turn? Give me the book. I will keep it well hidden." She reached up and caught at her sister's sleeve. With a cry of horror they saw the volume fall to the floor and though it was but seconds before it was covered by Anne Herbert's skirts, keen eyes had already seen.

Katherine looked up and met the full force of Lady Russell's gaze. Quickly she took the book beneath her own wide sleeves and defiantly returned the woman's icy stare. She couldn't be sure just how much the lady had seen, but from the calculating, almost triumphant expression in that face, it was sufficient.

The woman turned sharply away, her pearl stitched hood catching the light reflected from the torches high up on the walls as she moved into the shadows and lost herself in the crowd of young Maids of Honour.

"That Lady will cause mischief. Heaven knows we showed our guilt only too plainly. I must take my leave and conceal this somewhere at once before she can take her information to its destination. At least I cannot be charged with treason without proof, and as yet she has none. At least none save what her malicious clacking tongue can tell."

"It may be enough, Madam." Anne Herbert's mouth trembled. "Dear God, I will never forgive myself if I have brought about your downfall by my own stupidity. If only I could believe she has no evidence which will condemn you."

Generously Katherine put an arm about her. "Dear child, even I cannot be condemned merely for possessing a book. Lady Russell knows nothing of its nature. Now believe me, no harm is done. If they are so determined to be rid of me they will have other, more subtle methods than this, you may be sure." She rose to her feet. "I think we must move, Anne. There are too many restless people waiting to have words with me. They will think it strange if I sit in this corner with my sister. Perhaps I can make some excuse, if I could delay them and Lady Russell until I have hidden this safely away."

Slowly she drew her sister into the centre of the hall again.

"Ladies, come gather round. We shall have some music. Lady Russell, you will play the lute, if you please, and Lady Herbert and little Jane Grey shall sing for you. One of the King's own compositions." She watched as they fluttered to seat themselves in a circle, and reassuringly patted her sister's hand. "Cease your fretting, Anne. Even the Bishop will never have the King's consent to search my own apartments. The book will be safe there."

The woman responded with a half smile, then took her place at the centre of the circle. They waited patiently for the Queen to be seated, but she waved them on.

"I shall join you later. I must first visit the Princesses, so pray continue without me."

Lady Russell's eyes flickered upwards and then away again in a frown of displeasure. Her lips tightened into a malicious line of hatred. Ah well, the Bishop may not be free to search the Queen's apartments, but who would think to suspect one of the Queen's own women? A smile of satisfaction gave her a devilish look as she watched the fast retreating figure of Katherine.

THIRTEEN

"MORE TALES of treason, Gardiner?" Henry roared. Vigorously he snatched a heavy chain of gold set with rubies from a casket and placed it unceremoniously about his immense shoulders. "Don't you know I'm wearied beyond the point of endurance with them." With an effort he heaved himself out of the chair and dragged his tormented limbs to a softer, padded couch. The design of the rich fabric had been worked by the two princesses some years earlier, and Mary had ruefully complained that the material for it had cost some twenty pounds from her privy purse. Considering the vast proportions of the couch, it did not seem inconceivable.

Henry's face was now grey and tinged with dots of perspiration. A cry of pain escaped him as he lifted the leg on to a footstool. Gardiner watched in silence, pity long ago banished by contempt.

"I'll not waste your time with mere stories, Sire. Your Grace asked for proof of the Queen's treason and I have it." Almost triumphantly he said it, and Henry's bloated face stared back at him blankly.

"And when did I ask for evidence against the Queen, Gardiner?" He said it a shade too rapidly. "Have I given you reason to suppose that I am not content with my wife?" His grey eyes narrowed as he peered at the Bishop. Beneath his enormous padded doublet his heart began to beat furiously. Evidence against Kate? Surely the man lied. This was a pattern too often played in the past for him not to recognise it.

Gardiner flushed. He had made the error of forgetting that the King must never be blamed for any unpleasant act.

"Of course Your Grace did not ask for evidence against the Queen, but your ministers have a certain duty, Sire, and when such things are discovered it is their task to protect the King against it, from wherever it may come."

Henry preferred to hear it expressed thus and he relaxed a little.

"We can find no fault in that, my Lord, but to the question of the Queen our wife . . . that were something we find difficult to believe, that she should be guilty of so grave an act. We know her to be a good woman, Gardiner, an honest woman. We are not sure that we wish to hear of this evidence." He sank back into the couch, pulling towards him the mirror held by his barber. In it he scruitinised the swollen, flabby face and grimaced. Furiously he pushed the man away as if he were to blame for what he saw there. "Possibly you are mistaken, Bishop?" He turned to stare at Gardiner. "If you were to think again . . ."

Gardiner did indeed begin to have qualms about this business. If the King were still determined to protect the Queen it made his task so much more difficult and dangerous. Could it be that he had underestimated Katherine's power? He pulled himself together. Such an opportunity would not arise again. Lady Russell had found that damning evidence concealed among Katherine's private papers. She had done as he asked and had brought it to him. If he now failed to use it, Katherine would forever retain that hold upon the King and might even in time persuade him to her own way of thinking. He shuddered and pulled his long robe about him.

"I would be failing in my duty if I hid this evidence, Your Grace."

"We can close our eyes when necessary, Bishop," Henry replied peevishly. "The Queen is a good woman."

Gardiner squirmed at the insistent repetition. "That was my belief also, Your Grace, until this matter came to light. Now, reluctant as I am, love for my King forces me to disregard fear of your anger. I must present the facts to you, distasteful as they are."

"I might choose to dispute that love for your King, Gardiner." Henry glowered. "I have warned you that you risk our displeasure."

"But Your Grace was ever a generous and merciful King. I am assured of a fair hearing."

Henry straightened up. "That is true, my Lord. No one can say that Harry of England denied a fair hearing to any man. Present your evidence and we shall decide for ourselves whether it is justified or not." Clearly his face implied doubt, for he laughed. Well, let him laugh. It would be short lived.

The Bishop moved forward and withdrew from his robe a small book. With an almost insolent air he laid it casually upon the table at the King's side. His hand tapped rhythmically upon it and he watched the first glimmer of uncertainty come to Henry Tudor's face.

"If it is forbidden for commonfolk to read literature such as this, then can it be any less so for the Queen?" A slight thrill of exhilaration passed over him as he saw first doubt and then anger show itself in the King's eyes.

Henry's fist came down heavily on the volume and reluctantly he began to thumb through its pages, sucking his breath in sharply through his teeth.

"Tyndale's book." He seemed to find it difficult to say.

"Yes, Your Grace. A book full of the vilest heresies, for which reason it was justly banned. Can you permit the reading of such a work? Will you see your people subjected to it and not raise a hand to protect them from themselves? Sire, they are innocent fools." He rushed on now, warming to his argument. "Innocent, ignorant fools who follow like sheep any traitor who dares to encourage them away from the true Church."

Henry thrust the book away from him, turning away to cover his eyes with his hand. He was suddenly sickened by doubts. Was it possible? Could it be that Kate deceived him? He ridiculed the idea.

"We cannot believe the Queen to be guilty of such a crime, Bishop. Treason is a harsh word. Do you try to tell me that the King does not know his own wife? That it were possible for such treachery to be carried out under my very nose and I not to be aware of it?"

Gardiner raised his hands. "Women are subtle in such matters. Did the Queen not try to instruct your own children in this very same faith, knowing full well that it was against your own wishes?" He moved away from that keen gaze. "It would seem to me, Sire, that such disobedience were treason enough, but that the Queen, a woman raised to that position by Your Grace's own generosity, should encourage the people to doubt your own right as Supreme Head of the Church in England," he laughed scornfully, "why, that, Your Grace, is worse than any other crime."

Those grey eyes were suddenly colourless as chips of ice as Henry struggled with the incredible knowledge that he had been made to look a fool.

"I could not be so deceived in yet another Queen, Gardiner?" It was more a pathetic cry for reassurance.

"Lady Latimer has always seemed a true and loving wife ..."

"Can you be certain even of that, Sire?" Thin lips murmured the words softly with seeming reluctance.

Henry jerked forward with a cry of disbelief.

"What say you, Gardiner? Have a care."

"I say no more than many others in this court, Your Grace, that the Queen has outwitted the King. Has made him look a fool."

Violently Henry pushed back the couch and staggered to his feet, ignoring the cursed leg with almost superhuman effort. "God's blood, I'll have your neck, Gardiner. No man calls Henry Tudor a fool."

"Then you must also deal in like manner with the rest of Europe, Sire, for surely they, like your own people, are not blind to the fact that the Queen favours your Lord High Admiral with more than customary courtesy."

The King seemed almost to foam at the mouth. "You lie. You lie." He screamed the words, hammering his hand against the table, sending delicate Venetian glass hurtling to the floor in his unspeakable pain.

The Bishop eyed him sadly. "I could wish it were so, Your Grace, but surely you must know that Lord Seymour once had hopes of marrying the Queen?"

Quickly Henry turned away. Who better than he to know it? Was it not he who had separated the lovers? Guilt quickened his anger as always.

"Will you spare me nothing, Gardiner? Must I bear this as well as treason? I'll not believe the Queen guilty of adultery with my own brother-in-law. Why, I personally commanded the withdrawal of Lord Seymour from the court when I wed the lady. There has been no opportunity ..." He swung to face Gardiner and saw the discomfort in

129

the man's face. Ah, his heart seemed to beat less hurriedly for a moment. In this matter at least he could be sure of Kate. Gardiner would never find evidence to prove his accusation. His triumph was short lived, however.

"Your Grace was well advised to dismiss the High Admiral. His reputation is well known and even the Queen must be protected from such a man." He grasped at the excuse as a drowning man at a straw. "But her innocence in this will not excuse that other more vile crime of treason."

Henry's face darkened again. Why in God's name had she had to interfere in such things?

"The Queen knowingly gave refuge and comfort to the traitor Anne Askew. Mistress Askew openly supported the New Faith; it was for this that her husband and family forbade her the shelter of her own home. And who can blame them? They at least did not share her heretical beliefs, but the woman found sympathy enough in Queen Katherine."

"And what proof have you that Katherine gave the woman shelter?"

"The woman's own words, Sire." Gardiner froze for an instant as he spoke. Anne Askew had gone to the flames without naming any of her confidants, but one look at Henry's face told him that the lie had served its purpose, and what did it matter that it was a lie, so long as the Queen's treachery was discovered?

Henry's face contorted in a sudden spasm of agony. He limped away, groping blindly for the support of the window, sucking in his breath trying to stifle the sobs which forced their way up through his lips. Suddenly an old man, he lowered himself to the bench and for a few moments the apartment was filled only with the sound of his terrible anguish.

What had he done to deserve such treachery yet again?

"I raised her from nothing to be Queen of England, Gardiner. Surely if my Katherine were guilty of these crimes I would have seen, would have known? Is it possible she could repay me in this way ..."

The Bishop shrugged. "Your Grace is human, overly generous. The Lady has done nothing to warrant such kindness as she has thus far received at your hands."

"But I cannot believe it of Katherine." Tears fell unheeded onto the rich, padded fabric of Henry's doublet. "She was always so kind, so gentle ..."

Gardiner realised with sudden panic that even now the King might be foolish enough to forgive any sin in the Queen. "Is the day come, then, when Henry Tudor asks only pity from his wife? Does Harry of England forget how his people call him the 'golden King'." He bent close to Henry, uttering the words with as much scorn as he dared. "Does the King forget that any great alliance in Europe may be his?"

Henry ceased his lamentations, feeling suddenly enraged as he saw what he had almost allowed himself to become. A snivelling wreck of a man.

"What must I do, Gardiner? In God's name what must I do?"

The Bishop relaxed and sidled away. With apparent unconcern he stood by the writing desk, toying with a quill. "It is quite clear the Queen must be silenced before she can do real harm, otherwise I am much afeared this country will be brought to Civil War in its efforts to decide who truly rules England."

Panic rose in Henry's throat. "I have warned the Lady many times."

"Warnings are not sufficient deterrent, Sire. Stronger methods must be used."

"The Lady is still my wife."

"And has she shown herself worthy of that great estate?" Gardiner retaliated bluntly. "Where are your sons, Sire? Where indeed are the babes at all?" He laughed mirthlessly.

Henry winced. Dare he admit that sometimes he wondered if it might be he who was at fault? But that were surely not possible.

"The Queen contents herself with ministering to her husband as if he were an old man in his dotage, Your Grace. Why, there are so many new remedies, new potions, clearly the Lady thinks herself more capable than your own physicians. One might almost think she is obsessed with your ill health and waits only for a swift end." Gardiner hit cruelly now where it would strike the King most painfully, for Henry had ever been terrified by the thought of his own death. "And when the Lady is not so occupied, she spends her time in converting your people to her own beliefs. God's blood, Sire, it will not be long before the Queen rules here."

Henry's lips quivered. Bitterly he tried to shut out the memory of that beloved face. He still found it hard to believe that anyone as sweet, as innocent as Kate could be so treacherous. But Gardiner was right. It was he, Henry Tudor, who ruled England. No woman should ever look to take that right upon herself.

"But what can I do? She is still my wife, still a Queen."

"Queens have been removed before, Your Grace."

He flinched. Who knew it better than he? "This needs

to be thought on further. Six wives I have had, my Lord, and still only one son to show for it. Edward is frail. Can I leave England in such insecure hands, knowing that only Mary and Elizabeth remain? Heaven forbid that my people should come to be ruled by women."

Gardiner tapped his fingertips together and watched him closely. "Is it necessary to fear that possibility, Sire?"

Henry stared at him, uncomprehending. "But if the Queen were removed . . ."

"Then surely Your Grace intends to wed again."

The King's mouth fell open. He felt stunned by the possibility which had not occurred to him. "A seventh Queen?"

"And why not?" the smiling voice persuaded. "Surely Your Grace did not think himself past taking another wife?" The thin face reflected surprise. "Why, the King is still in his prime, a handsome figure of a man. I have seen for myself how the ladies clamour still for your favours. Forgive me, Sire, but it would seem the Queen has convinced you too well of your ill health."

Doubt began to give way to familiar conceit as Henry remembered that laughing young child in the gardens. The one who even now wore his ring. God's blood, she had challenged him saucily enough. He chuckled. Maybe Gardiner was right—a seventh Queen and perhaps even sons. Anything was possible with a young wife.

Suddenly he resented Kate. He remembered the sullen droop to her mouth, the arguments when she outbested him.

"I am persuaded your advice is good, Bishop. For England's sake the King must beget sons. Shall I fail the people who love me by denying them their right—Princes to continue the Tudor line? By our Lord," his hand smacked loudly against the oak panelling, "the Queen has shown herself no longer worthy of our love."

"Then it is for Your Grace to remedy a tragic situation."

"How, my Lord, how?" Henry waited as if for some miracle to release him.

Slowly Gardiner leaned across the desk and dipped the quill into an ink horn. From beneath his robe he withdrew a parchment and this he unrolled, placing it on the desk.

Curiosity brought Henry slowly to his side, gasping and wheezing, and there he stared down at that paper.

"You have but to sign this and all will be dealt with, swiftly and without fuss." He held the quill up. The King raised his hand, which trembled so violently that he couldn't grasp the instrument. Gently Gardiner steadied the swollen fingers, forcing them to tighten. Slowly he guided the King's hand down to the document.

For a moment he feared Henry might yet change his mind. Briefly other faces drifted through the King's head. Anne Boleyn, haughty and beautiful. Kathryn Howard, a child too young to die. He closed his eyes. They deserved to die.

The quill scratched loudly as he signed with a flourish the warrant for the arrest of Katherine Parr upon a charge of high treason.

FOURTEEN

IN HIS own rooms, Gardiner sat at his desk, scratching noisily with a quill upon the document before him. It held

134

the King's signature; the only further item to be added was Wriothesely's name as Chancellor. Thus were great ladies brought to an end ...

He rolled up the parchment and reached for a bell which lay close at hand. He waited patiently until a page answered his summons, standing before the huge desk, shivering in thin hose and jerkin.

"You will deliver this into the hands of the Chancellor, and mind," he warned, "if it should fall into the wrong hands you shall pay dearly for it, very dearly indeed." Bony fingers gently tapped the document on the desk as he stared at the boy.

The lad paled a little, wondering what could be of such import, but he bowed and said nothing. Tightly grasping that parchment, he withdrew, stepping into the cold, dimly lit passage beyond.

The court seemed strangely deserted that day. His footsteps echoed eerily on the stone floor and he shivered. It was almost as if he were the last soul left alive in this huge place. For a second he glanced behind him as if expecting a spirit to appear, then he laughed, a childish, high-pitched sound. Probably it was the November frost which kept the noble Lords and Ladies huddled close to their fires, and who could blame them? They were not hardened as he was to this bitter cold, to the cell-like rooms which were his quarters below stairs. Though on a day such as this when his belly rattled with hunger, he would have given much to sit at the big, crowded table, warmed by a good fire, and to fill himself with a portion of good, red beef, a hunk of bread, and swill it all down with a pint of ale.

He turned a corner and began to climb narrow, torch-lit stairs. Everywhere shadows hung, for sunlight seldom reached this part of the palace. From behind a thick oak door faint sounds of music drifted, and a smile touched his lips. It was reassuring to know that at least some person was still alive.

He paused, leaning against the wall, hoping to hear more of the tune. Then with a shrug he turned and sat on the cold stone steps, tucking his hands under his knees to keep them warm. His toes screwed up in the thin leather shoes and it was hard to keep his teeth from chattering, but it was worth a little discomfort to hear such music. The parchment lay at his side, momentarily forgotten.

For several minutes he remained thus, lost in thought and content to listen to the merry sounds which spilled from that room, until reluctantly he realised that someone was sure to pass this way very soon. He reached out for the document at his side, his mind still more than half with the occupants of that room. Idly he stared down at the parchment, glanced up and down the stairs furtively, then reached for it, tapping it gently against his knee. Hesitantly then, slowly, he began to unfurl the paper. After all, where was the harm?

For a moment he failed to understand, for words were still strange to him. But then his eyes grew wide as he stared again at them. His education had not been extensive but it was sufficient to enable him to slowly fathom the horrifying things written there, and what held him yet further was the fact that this dreadful paper was complete even to the large signature scrawled at the bottom.

Dots of clammy perspiration broke out on his young face. He actually felt sick, as with trembling hands he rolled the parchment tightly again. A warrant for the arrest of the Queen. He had seen such papers before in the Lord Chancellor's rooms, but never until now had they meant much to him. With a feeling of disgust he realised that he was to be the instrument of delivering so foul a despatch. He rose from the steps dizzily. So the King thought to rid himself of yet another wife? Was the monster never to be satisfied? Katherine Parr had always treated the lower members of her court with extreme kindness, aye, and one of his own younger brothers hoped to learn to read and write because of the Queen's concern and interest.

Blindly he stumbled up the stairs, his feet finding the well worn grooves. Well, not if he could prevent it would so great a lady meet her death at that creature's hands. Yet how to prevent it? He remembered Gardiner's warning as it echoed in his ears. "You shall pay dearly if this paper falls into the wrong hands."

He came to a lighter, more airy passage and stood shaking with fear, trying to decide what he must do. Suddenly from one of the rooms a young woman appeared. He recognised her vaguely as one of the Queen's women and, almost without realising it, his mind was made up. Quick as an arrow he darted forward, catching at her sleeve so that she started with fright. Swiftly he pushed the paper into her hands.

"Give this to the Queen, mistress, as quickly as you can, for her life is in terrible danger."

The woman stared after him as he ran away, confused by the fear she had seen in his young face. She unrolled the paper, staring down at it, and then she swayed, feeling the icy waves of horror grip her.

Somehow she managed to conceal the dreadful item, managed to fight her way dizzily back to the Queen's rooms. Almost fainting with fright, she ran straight to Katherine, pushing the warrant into her hands.

"Read, Madam, read," Lady Somers begged, weeping openly now.

"Heavens, child, what is it?" Katherine laughed uneasily as she did as she was bid.

Her ladies gathered silently round, watching in alarm as her face grew white as chalk. Whatever news the Queen read there must be alarming indeed, for with a strangled cry Katherine fell to the floor in a swoon.

The women hovered between the stricken Queen and the terrified knowledge that there was naught they might do to prevent this tragedy.

Anne Herbert's fingers clenched tightly as if she would tear the wretched warrant to shreds. Around her the ghostly faces watched, wide-eyed, willing her to do it and yet knowing that to perform the act would be to sentence them all to death.

With a sob Anne's hand fell. She raised tear-filled eyes to the heavens as if the measure of her grief alone might move some unknown angel to mercy.

"Dear God, if I thought for one moment it would save her I would burn that despicable thing and die gladly for it." She stumbled blindly away from Lady Somers' arms when that woman would have held her.

"Would we not all, Anne, a thousand times over?"

"We will not save the Queen by keeping the warrant from its destination. That is certain." Jane Grey bit her pink, childish lip uncertainly. "Bishop Gardiner will expect Chancellor Wriothesely to carry out the King's command, and if my Lord does not, then he will swiftly want to know the reason for it."

"Aye, Jane is right. It would not take long for Gardiner's wily mind to sense that something is wrong, and he would know straightway where to come. We cannot expect the young man, his messenger, to suffer the questioning which its disappearance will entail. He dared more than enough by coming to us with this warrant. But if the Bishop discovered how we had dealt with an order of the King's own hand I'll wager our heads and that of the Queen would grace Tower Bridge before morning."

A deadly silence fell as they looked at each other, waiting for some impossible solution to offer itself. It was Margaret Neville who spoke at last, quietly uttering the words they were each afraid to say.

"We have no choice. The warrant must be delivered. All we may hope is that some miracle occurs in the few hours before the Chancellor can act upon it."

There were silent nods.

"But how can we deliver it now?"

"Alas, child, that is the easiest part. Any page will carry it. Wriothesely knows not one from the other. I could but wish the rest were as simple."

Jane Grey's eyes filled with tears, like large pansies suddenly drenched in a shower of rain. She stood in silence, her plump little hands clasped upon her gown, feeling confused and utterly helpless as the older women sobbed desolately around her. It was as if they thought she could not understand their grief, and she longed to cry aloud that despite her nine years she too could not bear to lose so dear a friend.

FIFTEEN

DEMENTED SOBS issued forth from he Queen's bedchamber.

Katherine lay shaking with fear upon the velvet coverlet,

the beautiful gown of green and silver crushed carelessly by her slender body, since her women had not yet been able to calm her sufficiently in order to remove it. The long dark hair escaped from her hood, becoming wet with tears, and still she wept and screamed.

Around the bed her women wept in each other's arms, all save Lady Russell, who busied herself at the far end of the room. Bewildered and stunned, none could yet believe the terrible blow which had befallen them. It couldn't be true that the King would so cruelly rid himself of yet another wife, and surely not one so well beloved as Katherine Parr.

Yet every one of them had read for herself that terrible warrant. It was not imagination which caused the Queen to swoon and then become as a mad woman, screaming and tearing at her hair.

"It is a lie," she moaned helplessly. "The King would not do this to me. There is some mistake, a terrible mistake."

But there was no mistake. That warrant was even now in Wriothesely's hands. Every second they dreaded to hear the marching of feet which warned of the guards' coming.

Hysterically, Katherine turned her face into the pillows, trying to stifle her cries of terror which surely must reach every corner of the Palace, but all too clear was the picture of herself mounting the steps of the scaffold, of lowering her head to the block. Mercifully she fainted again.

Lady Herbert fought to bring her own feelings under control. Her heart pounded with fear and she felt physically sick. Dear God, the King had much to answer for. Tight lipped, she straightened up from the bed where Katherine lay still as death.

"Ladies, we must do something. The Queen is ill, driven almost to the point of death by her terror. We cannot stand by much longer and do nothing, or I fear for her sanity."

Lady Russell folded a veil and surveyed her with malicious humour. "Why waste your time? The end will be the same. You can do nothing for her now."

Violently Anne Herbert advanced upon her. "This is your doing, Mistress. 'Tis you brought the Queen within the shadow of the block, and for what? A book, a book which could do no harm. Some day . . . some day I swear you shall be sorry." Only with the greatest effort did she prevent herself from striking the woman.

"It was treason. She deserves to die." The thin face reddened with defiance.

" 'Tis you who deserves to die." Lady Somers wept. "If there is any treason here then 'tis yours, and pray God you pay dearly for it."

Katherine dimly heard the raised voices and as the word treason edged its way into her senses, screams again rose to her lips. It was as if they came from some other body than her own.

Quickly Anne Herbert turned and went to her sister. She bathed the clammy, pale face with scented water and ordered fresh logs to be put on the fire. Katherine seemed to shiver uncontrollably.

"This will do no good." Reluctantly Anne admitted the fact, straightening up. "I must fetch the physician. He at least might calm her a little, otherwise I fear she will simply die of fright."

"I fear for my own sanity if this nightmare does not end soon. Poor Queen, poor generous Queen." Lady Rivers buried her face in her hands and stumbled away from the bed.

Anne took a last look at her sister, brushed the tears away from her own cheeks and straightened her gown.

"I will fetch Doctor Wendy now. Lady Jane Grey, if you will sit beside the bed in case she wakens. The rest of you stay close at hand and bar the doors against the King's guard. Even they will not dare to drag her from her bed by force, I think." Her amber gown whirled as she sped away.

The draughty passages seemed never-ending as she ran in search of that tiny room. "Please, God, let him not refuse me," she whispered as she stumbled on. Her foot caught in the hem of her gown and she almost fell, grazing her hand against the wall, yet she did not feel it. Breathlessly she leaned for a moment, gasping and choking against the stonework before pushing open the door.

"Doctor, please come. Please come, the Queen is in sore need of you."

The old man's face wrinkled with concern. "Is she ill? I heard nothing."

"This illness was very sudden to strike, Doctor," Lady Herbert gasped. "But I beg you to come quickly, or I very much fear it will be too late."

Without hesitation the old man collected several items and shuffled after her. His leather shoes grated and scraped over the flagstones, his breath came in short wheezing gasps as he struggled to keep up with the woman. She ushered him unceremoniously into the royal bedchamber, and when he would have wasted time making his bows she dragged him forward to the bed with a cry of impatience.

"The Queen does not see you, Doctor. She'll not reprove you for any lack of formality this time."

The old man bent over Katherine, peering short-sightedly at the chalk-white face. Long dark lashes fanned onto her cheeks as she lay unmoving. He frowned. "For how long has she been like this?"

"Several hours. Sometimes she wakens, but only to begin screaming. Horrifying, tormented sounds." Anne Herbert watched as he laid a hand over Katherine's heart and little Jane Grey moved silently away from the bed to stand in the shadows. Her lips trembled with pity for the unfortunate Queen. What a terrible fate it was for any woman to rise to such state.

"I should have been called earlier." Doctor Wendy cut in upon their thoughts.

Guiltily the women lowered their eyes. "We were afraid to summon help, doctor. We were afraid you would not come."

"Not come?" He looked up in amazement. "It is my duty to attend the Queen." The very thought seemed to shock him.

"But can you help her?"

He considered that, tugging at his short, grey beard. "I don't know. This is a most unusual illness. Something I have not seen the like of before . . ." He faltered. "Or perhaps I have though 'tis rare." The shrewd eyes pierced Lady Herbert's face and she flushed. Gently he took her arm and drew her away from the bed. "Tell me what occurred prior to the Queen's illness."

"I don't understand."

He smiled. "Mistress, I think you do. Let me tell you that only twice before have I seen a similar illness, and in each case the ladies had reason enough to wish an easy death, or at least an escape from life."

Anne 's hand flew to her mouth. "Easy death? In God's name, what are you saying?"

"The first was Queen Anne. The Boleyn, when she learned that she was accused of treason. The second was Kathryn Howard in a like situation. Aye, that one ran

143

screaming through the palace like a mad thing." His old eyes watched for her reaction and he saw her sway. "I see I am not mistaken?"

Tears welled up again in her eyes as she shook her head. "We feared you would not risk the King's displeasure by attending Her Grace."

"I think, Mistress, the King would not deny this Queen the services of her doctor. He is not so ruthless a man, really."

"I wonder you can say it when he condones yet another murder, sends another wife to the block."

His face was wreathed with lines. "I know little of the King's affairs. Rumour reaches me, people talk; they think because I am old that I hear nothing. If there is any dispute between the King and his wife it is because of her interest in the New Faith."

"The Queen risked his anger many times in order to defend her beliefs, yet we did not think he was so angered that he would go this far."

"I wonder even now if this is truly the King's doing."

"Why should you doubt it?" Her voice was shrill with hysteria and the doctor patted her hand gently.

"Because, my Lady, the King grows old. He'll not admit it, of course, but there comes a time when even a King must accept the facts. He had reconciled himself to his wife, was pleased by her charm, her humility and above all by her gentleness. These gifts he would not throw away lightly unless he was persuaded to it in one of those weak moments of resentment which we all know befall the King. He is not to be blamed, Lady Herbert. If any should take that responsibility, then look to the King's Bishop."

"Wherever the blame lies, doctor, that warrant is signed. It bears the King's name plainly enough."

"But it is possible that he might even now regret that signature."

She stared at him. "You hope for too much, Sir. The damage is done."

"We shall see." Casually he prepared a small posset for the Queen. "Give her this and leave the rest to me. One way or another we shall have the answer." Then he was gone.

In bitter despair they could only sit helplessly by, surrounding the great bed. Watching the lifeless form and weeping silently.

An hour passed and still no one moved. Suddenly the door was pushed open. It fell with a crash against the wall. Immediately all eyes turned to stare as if expecting to see the palace guard, and then the women fell into deep curtseys as Henry's great frame advanced painfully into the bedchamber.

He scarcely noticed them as he made his way to the bed. Silently they drew back, watching and waiting with stilled breath. For a moment he stood looking down at the pale, almost unreal face. His mouth trembled and quickly he went down onto his knees, grasping the Queen's tiny hand into his own.

"Kate," he whispered. "Kate, it is Hal."

There was no response. Still she lay as if dead and he frowned, becoming more alarmed.

"Kate, I am here, sweetheart. 'Tis Harry."

"She does not hear Your Grace," Anne advised him gently.

Henry looked at her as if she were crazed. "Not hear? But she must hear." An arm went swiftly beneath Katherine's shoulders and he held her up close to him. The long black hair trailed over his arm, caressing the pillows. "Kate, it is Hal. You must speak to me, sweetheart."

"Alas, the Queen suffers some terrible shock, Your Grace." Doctor Wendy moved closer to the bed. "Some terror closes her mind to all reality. It is as if she were dead."

Henry's face crumpled. "Dead? My Kate? Why should she die, man? What has she done that she should deserve to die?" Angrily he confronted the doctor.

"I know nothing of the cause, Your Grace. I only know the symptoms. The Queen is mortally afraid and unless she receives some reassurance, then she will surely die."

Guilt flooded Henry's bloated face. It was he had done this to Kate. Because of him she lay close to death. Suddenly she was once again the thing he desired most, the lovely creature he had married. Dear Lord, what had he done? Why had he allowed Gardiner to persuade him to sign that warrant? Gardiner was to blame for this; he convinced himself of that, and by the Lord, if aught should happen to Kate then the Bishop would pay dearly for it.

Tears glistened on his lashes as gently he kissed her ice cold cheek. Her dark hair spilled silkily over her shoulders and he caressed it gently, suddenly terrified that she might leave him alone again. "Kate, you must come back to me, sweetheart," he sobbed. "Come back to Hal, who needs you and loves you. There is some mistake, the warrant was signed by mistake . . . it was Gardiner's error and he shall pay for it." He murmured the words as she could hear. "The King wants you, Kate. He begs you not to die. Our life would be empty if you went away."

Weeping bitterly now, he laid his head against her hand. Behind him the women sobbed with relief and Anne

146

Herbert's eyes voiced her silent gratitude to the doctor, who simply smiled and withdrew.

Through a haze Katherine was suddenly aware of a heavy weight pressing against her. In sudden panic she imagined it to be her coffin and she cried out, screaming against it. Hands held her firmly, securely. She rested warmly against a body which shook and trembled and spilled salt tears onto her face.

"She is come back to me. The Queen is come back to me."

It was Henry's voice. Weakly she pulled away and looked up at him and was amazed to see the grief in his face.

"Your Grace." Her dry lips formed the words.

"Kate if you had gone from me my life would have come to an end." He cradled her in his arms.

"But I thought you wished my arrest, the warrant . . ." She felt utterly confused.

" 'Twas nothing sweetheart. A mistake. Gardiner's doing. Put it from your mind sweet, he shall pay for such treachery."

"I thought I had displeased Your Grace. That I was to be punished because of my interest in the New Learning, yet I swear to you I intended no treason."

"I know it sweetheart, I know it."

"If I argued with Your Grace it was merely to divert you, to take your mind from the pain . . ." Still she struggled to reassure him.

"My gentle nurse, what would I do without you?"

She could scarcely believe the nightmare was over. That she had escaped the trap laid so cleverly for her. Tears of relief fell rapidly and it was the King who brushed them away.

God's blood how could he have listened to Gardiner's malice? How could he have believed ill of Kate who loved him so much?

Footsteps rang loudly in the passage beyond. Instantly her fears returned. Her women screamed and huddled together as the door fell open. Wriothesely marched in triumphantly followed by a guard of some twenty men.

"I am come in the King's name to arrest you upon a charge of High Treason Madam." He addressed himself to the limp, weeping figure who fell to sobbing again.

From where he stood, Henry seemed to grow by a foot as his fury mounted. Hands on hips he swayed in his anger, watching the miserable Chancellor through narrowed eyes.

"You fool." He bellowed. "Imbecile. Get out."

Wriothesely backed in alarm and his men retreated in a huddle. "But Your Grace, the warrant it was signed . . ." He floundered helplessly before that terrifying giant.

"There has been some terrible error and those responsible shall pay for it. How dare you subject the Queen of England to such treachery? Get out my Lord Chancellor or you shall quickly find another such warrant bearing your own name. Get out I say." He advanced upon the startled man with amazing speed for one of his proportions. Yet still quicker was the Chancellor who beat a hasty retreat, realising that something had gone seriously amiss.

From her bed Katherine could only laugh and weep at the same time, and gradually Henry's face changed from anger to boyish innocence as he hobbled to the bed again.

"There you see Kate. I saved you from the madman did I not?"

Dizzily she held out her hand to him and he knelt beside the bed. Gently she stroked the pale golden hair, smiling above his head to her ladies. They withdrew silently.

"Yes indeed you saved me from the madman Henry." She murmured. Yet how long before they begin to work again upon your moods and I am once again living in fear of every shadow?

SIXTEEN

"The King has ordered the arrest of Norfolk, Madam." Lady Somers stabbed half-heartedly at her needlework, glancing up at Katherine.

The Queen rested her own work upon her knee and sighed. "Has he so? Well I confess it does not surprise me. The King jumps at shadows these days, and if he has reason to fear anyone, then it is Norfolk who was ever ambitious." She reached for a strand of green silk and matched it to her embroidery.

Lady Somers frowned and the rest of the women listened intently to this item of gossip.

"My Lord of Norfolk did well to escape with his life after his niece Kathryn Howard went to the block, so that I can understand the King's anger remaining even now. But his son, the Earl of Surrey . . . why cause this young man to be committed to the Tower?"

"I did hear that he was charged with quartering the Arms of Edward the Confessor with the emblem of his own House." Little Jane Grey volunteered, and Katherine smiled down at the child who sat at her feet.

"It is little enough sin. Hardly treason I think Jane."

The child pursed her tiny lips, intently studying her neat stitches."

"We know how easily all things may be construed as treason when it is politic to have them so Madam I think."

The older women looked sharply at each other over her head, and though Katherine began to speak, she closed her lips again on the words, realising what truth lay in the words.

"There are many versions of the story flying about the court as always Madam." Lady Tyrwhitt began almost apologetically. "But perhaps I have the truest of all. The Howards still have much influence in England by reason of the marriage of their two nieces to the King. True, Norfolk is forbidden the court, but one cannot undo those marriages. It irks them more than a little I'll wager to be so out of favour, whilst the King looks so kindly upon my Lord Hertford and the rest of the Seymours(who will undoubtedly one day become guardians to the young Prince. My Lord Hertford is after all uncle to the Prince, brother to the late Queen Jane."

"Indeed, as are all the Seymours." Katherine put in quietly, thinking of Thomas.

Lady Tyrwhitt nodded. "What more natural then than that these good men should have guardianship of the King's son? But my Lord Surrey obviously thinks otherwise. Foolishly he dared to threaten to have his revenge for being thus deprived of that power which might have been his, had he been the one to assume protection of the Prince when he comes to the throne. He spoke openly threatening the life of Lord Hertford."

Katherine stared at her in bewilderment. "This is the first I have heard of any suggestion that the Howards should have charge of Edward."

"Indeed it is the first any have heard of it Madam, until it leaked out that Surrey had boasted of his intentions when he came into control of the new King."

"But this is scandalous news." Katherine threw down her work and rose to her feet. "The King would never give Edward into the hands of that family who were ever known Papists."

"Exactly so Madam. The Duke of Norfolk and his son made a grave error in threatening one of the Prince's guardians. His Grace jumps to protect in one move both his son and my Lord Hertford, by arresting the conspirators upon a charge of high treason."

"And God be praised he did so. Heaven forbid that this kingdom should fall into Norfolk's hands."

"Sir Thomas Seymour has taken care to see that such a possibility shall never occur Madam. What more natural than that he should fly to the side of his brother Lord Hertford and at the same time to the defence of the King's son. It was he first gathered news of the plot to control the next King."

Katherine turned away. "He is a brave man. well loved by the King. We owe him much."

"Aye Madam. Better were England beneath such hands than Norfolk's."

"Have you learned yet what is to become of the prisoners?"

"Only that the Duchess of Norfolk has been questioned concerning her husband's activities Madam, and the Duchess of Richmond, Surrey's sister likewise."

"And they were never women given to generous acts." Katherine put in quietly. "I'll wager they condemned their menfolk without any qualms of conscience?"

"They declared themselves to be the King's most humble

151

subjects, having no part in the plotting and wickedness of their kinfolk." Lady Tyrwhitt replied. "But I think no evidence of treason could be found in the house which was thoroughly searched."

"I doubt that any such lack of proof will deter the King." The Queen said it as if unconcerned, having learned well enough the King's determination.

"So it would seem Madam, since the Duke and his son are found guilty of the charge. Of quartering their own arms with those of the Confessor, thus aspiring however mistakenly to the throne. It is as we all know but a means of ridding the King of yet another insecurity."

"I could almost pity them, were it not for the knowledge that my own neck would not be safe for long once the Howards had worked upon Edward's innocent mind. They are Papists which I shall never be, and pray God Edward shall never be."

"Thanks to your own good influence and that of his uncles the Seymours, Madam." Lady Somers ventured.

"Yet it grieves me to see men go to the block for their beliefs, whoever they may be."

Jane Grey's large eyes met the Queen's with childlike frankness.

" 'Tis them or you Madam."

Katherine smiled. "I realise that Jane, and in any event I'll not be so unwise as to interfere again in matters which touch upon the King's conscience. If he is decided to condemn the Howards, there is nothing I may do to change it. We all know His Grace is not long for this world. I must remain content to have escaped with my life, and if only for Edward's sake I shall tread more warily in future, so that perhaps one day, from all of this will come a happier time."

Heads nodded in silent agreement, though it was hard to imagine the day would ever come when Henry Tudor's shadow was lifted from England.

SEVENTEEN

THE KING'S bedchamber was tightly guarded against intruders. Within the room, windows were covered by black velvet hangings, giving an eerie, ghostly look to everything. A fire blazed in the huge hearth and heat rolled in waves, mingling with the stench of rotting decayed flesh and death. This latter had its own distinctive odour.

Men stood in silent groups watching the figure in the great bed. All through the night the King had gasped for breath and wept with the pain in his limbs. The physicians knew him to be close to death, yet none dared impart this news to the King, even now fearing to find themselves arrested on a charge of high treason for daring to predict the Sovereign's death.

"He sinks fast now my Lord."

"Any other man would have been well gone afore this." A figure in the shadows nodded agreement. "All night the palace has listened to his agony. God knows I'd not wish such torment as he suffers upon my worst enemy. He longs for death yet it seems to linger just beyond his reach, as if to torment him."

William Grenville's eyes strained to pierce the gloom as he watched the figure in the bed. "Think you England will mourn when dawn comes and the Tudor is gone?"

"Will England realise just what his death means? 'Tis the end of an era, of a time which will be remembered throughout history. Aye and I'll wager that's how Harry Tudor would have it, if the choice were his now. They will mourn right enough. Remembering his youth and how they loved him then. Forgetting with human generosity what he became these past years." The shadowed figure paused, shaking his head a little. "Rome will rejoice. The Pope has found Henry of England a persistent thorn in his flesh. At least now he can lick the wound and be sure that his enemy will not leap back to threaten the Catholic Church again with his wavering and denials."

"You forget my friend, the King's son will have none of Rome either. Edward is Protestant like the Queen, so that Rome cannot rejoice too much in his passing I think."

"Aye, but who follows Edward my Lord? Have you given thought to that? Ask yourself for how long will England remain Protestant when such as Mary Tudor hover close to the throne."

They studied each other in silence, both troubled by visions of a future England. They watched the physicians fluttering around the bed, helpless yet anxious to appear as if they did indeed work some miracle and would bring the King back to health even now.

"I can think of one who must wish the King had gone to his Maker in greater haste." William Grenville murmured.

"You mean Norfolk?"

"Who else? The King roused himself once during the night to put his hand to a warrant for Norfolk's execution which is to take place tomorrow, unless some miracle occurs at this late hour to prevent it."

"It may not be too far beyond the bounds of probability

154

yet Grenville . . . If the King should die before the order is acted upon."

"But would you exchange places with Norfolk this night, knowing that your own life depended upon how long it takes the King to quit his own?"

"God forbid, but then my ambition never equalled Norfolk's."

"The King will put his hand to no more such documents I think, for since then he has slipped steadily further away from life. Remember how in August he appointed Sir Anthony Denny, Mister Gate and Mister Clere to sign in his stead all warrants and official documents, yet still required that such papers needed his own signature to be attached? Well even were any further warrants to be prepared, the King could no longer raise the pen to give his name to them. How ironic that he should condemn Norfolk with his final act."

"Sir Anthony Denny looks mightily troubled, standing in the corner there, wringing his hands."

Grenville's lips curved in a wry smile. "And so would I if it fell to me to acquaint my Sovereign with news of his impending death. It was ever the one thing Henry could never accept, the knowledge that even he must one day loose his hold on life."

Bishop Gardiner remained in the shadows afraid to be seen lest Henry should come to his senses sufficiently long enough to order his arrest. Perhaps he might even now have found himself despatched to the Tower had not the King suddenly fallen ill, and even if Henry should die, he still had cause to tremble for his future. The young Prince Edward would have none of the Catholics. Thomas Seymour and his family had seen to that, aided by the Queen.

The boy was more Protestant than his besotted father realised.

Katherine Parr entered the bedchamber silently now. Those present bowed but she hardly saw them. Her gaze was fixed intently upon that bed.

Sir Anthony Denny went to her side and whispered something.

"Someone must tell the King that he is close to death Madam. He may wish to see his spiritual Advisers."

She nodded, understanding and fighting back the lump in her throat. It was difficult to believe that the great Tudor had reached his final battle. Wryly she smiled. This fight at least was one he must surrender.

"You wish me to tell the King?" She questioned, and the man sighed with relief.

"Your word he will accept Madam. There is little time. We dare not leave it much longer."

"Don't worry, I will tell him my Lord."

Slowly she advanced to the great bed and knelt beside the King. She felt cold suddenly despite the heavy black velvet of her gown. His eyes were closed. Lines of pain had slipped from his face and he seemed suddenly a young man. For the first time she saw him as he once was, and her heart bled. Why had he become a lecher, the violent ruthless Monarch he was today?

Her hand rested on his against the coverlet as she knelt motionless there, trying to fathom the secrets of her husband. Had those other marriages been happier would he have been a different man? She realised not. There were always too many ambitious men surrounding a King. Were it not for such men Catherine of Aragon might have remained the first and only wife of Henry VIIIth. But always there would have been that desperate fanatical longing for a son. She pressed her hands together, supporting her head against them. Well he had his son. Jane's son. A frail lad, too young to be weighed down by the crown of England. But at least Edward would have Thomas Seymour to watch over him. This much at least Henry had promised.

From the corner of her eye she saw Gardiner and her eyes met his through the dim light. Her chin jerked defiantly upwards.

"I loved my husband in my own way." She longed to shout it. "He was a good man, a kind man." But again the thought came to her that if the King had not come to this sudden end, he might even now be signing yet another warrant for her arrest. Content to send her to the block because he could be so easily swayed by loathsome men such as the Bishop.

The hand moved slightly and she leaned forward.

"Henry."

His eyes flickered open. She thought he recognised her for he smiled, but the name upon his lips was that of Anne and she froze. So he still thought of the Boleyn. Ah well, perhaps it was guilt which rose to torment him and she could do nothing to ease that.

"Henry." She repeated, and he seemed to focus more clearly upon her face.

"Kate." The word was barely audible. "I thought you were gone from me."

"I am here my love as always when you need me."

His hand tightened momentarily on hers with surprising strength. He tried to turn his head, to look at her face but the effort was too much and he lay still, weeping silently with pain and frustration.

Katherine lowered her head to the coverlet, still pressing

his cold hand to her cheek. Salt tears fell to the fingers and Henry stirred himself again, bewildered by her grief.

"Nay Kate sweetheart. Don't weep for Hal. I brought you no great joy that you should be sad to see me go, and yet I did love you right well Kate, right well."

Her dark hair fell across their joined hands as she lifted her head.

"Then I beg you don't deny me these tears Henry, for I loved you too."

He was silent for a moment, his thoughts wandering. Caught in a dizzily spinning whirl of unreality. He cursed silently, realising that though he spoke, to the listening mourners the words were often a mere jumble of phrases. It took every last failing ounce of concentration to force the things he wanted to say to his lips, instead of the meaningless rambles which bubbled up.

A dark shape still hovered close to the bed. He stared at it intently with glassy eyes and seemed to shiver.

"Go from me Nan. Be done with your torment." His parched lips cried the phrase and he choked on the congestion in his throat. The dark shape moved. A cold hand brushed across his fevered brow and he relaxed again. "I meant you no harm Nan. Must you haunt me even now?"

"It is not Anne, Henry." A voice whispered softly, brokenly. " 'Tis Kate."

The swollen hand jerked and she moved closer so that his eyes might better focus upon her face.

"Aye 'tis Kate. My mind moves from one thing to another so swiftly. Death makes a blubbering idiot of me sweetheart."

"We are all brought to it one day my love. He is no respecter of persons."

He made a futile gesture with his hand. The other

158

clasped feebly at the restraining covers which seemed to hold him back from something . . . someone.

"Have you anything to tell us Henry? Is there aught you would say?"

The gentle voice urged him to consciousness again.

He thought on it as the minutes sped by. There were so many things . . . aye but was there time? He must find a husband for Mary. A suitable match. He frowned. There was Nan's child too, ah but that one, she would take care of herself.

"Edward." The sound rasped from his dry mouth urgently. "Look to Edward for me Kate. He is such a child to be left to the men in this court."

"Rest easy Henry. You know I shall care for him as if he were my own son."

"But you know so little of their ways Kate, the villainy . . ."

"I think I know enough, and I am strong. Besides you have already assured your son's safety by giving him into the protection of his uncles. No one could love Edward more Henry. He will come to no harm."

"It needs more than love to keep a King safe upon his throne sweetheart. Edward hasn't even experienced life yet. God's blood he is no more than a babe. Must I leave him to their mercies? Must I leave him?" His voice rose stunning the watching crowd into sudden fear. None would have put it past Henry Tudor to defy his Maker even now, for the sake of his son. But the huge mountain of flesh was quiet again. Such problems were no longer of importance. All that mattered was to be gone. Free of the pain, out of the misery which was life.

Again the voice jogged him into wakefulness.

"Henry there is little time. Will you see anyone?"

For a moment it seemed he did not hear, then he roused himself.

"Only Cranmer."

She nodded and rose from her knees. Already he had sunk into oblivion again.

Half an hour later the sound of the death rattle filled the bedchamber. The Queen stood watching, knowing that nothing was to be done, and then suddenly . . . silence. Strange, echoing silence.

A weight seemed to be lifted in that moment from Katherine's shoulders. Blankly she gazed down at the figure.

"He is gone Madam." Sir Anthony Denny touched her arm and she jumped.

"Yes my Lord, he finds peace at last." She moved away from the bed and walked out into the clearer, fresher air of the passages. She breathed deeply, lifting her face to the light cool air.

Without realising it, her step quickened. Men and women regarded her pityingly, weeping for the still young Dowager Queen, and all the time her brain shouted. The King is dead. Henry Tudor is gone and I am still alive. Her face was composed, deathly pale as she moved forward. Wind whipped at the black gown, lifted the veil which covered her hair.

Why do you weep? She longed to cry. The King is dead. Long live Katherine Parr.

She pressed her hands to her mouth as if afraid that hysterical laughter would bubble forth from her lips, and still the court watched her with eyes full of pity.

If only you knew, she thought. If only you knew what joy it is to be alive. Yet how could they? For surely only a wife who had managed to outlive the great Tudor could know such a feeling . . .